Cuddling in Clover Creek

At the Altar Series
A Clover Creek Story
Kirsten Osbourne

Sign up for instant notification of all of Kirsten's New Releases
http://www.kirstenandmorganna.com/newsletter

Chapter One

Sarah Walters wiped her hands on a kitchen cloth and hurried to the phone when it rang. It was her first anniversary and her husband, Doug, was due home any minute. She'd spent the last few hours making an extremely difficult supper to share the occasion with him—barefoot and pregnant in the kitchen, something she'd claimed she would never be.

Grabbing her cell, she put it to her ear, having seen it was Doug on the caller ID. "Hey, you," she said in her most sultry voice. It was hard to feel sexy when you were five months pregnant, but she did her best.

"Hey, Spook. The guys and I are going out for a few beers. Don't wait supper on me. I'll get a burger at the bar."

All of the excitement she'd felt throughout the day fell at her husband's words. "But…I made a special supper for our anniversary."

"Oh, was that today, babe? I thought it was next month." Doug paused for a moment. "I promised the guys. It's been forever since we just hung out together."

"Or last night…" She tried to keep the frustration from her voice, but there was no question in her mind. The guys would win, and she'd spend the night alone, eating a romantic supper for one.

"Don't get like that. You can't take your stupid pregnancy hormones out on me." Doug was obviously getting annoyed, and she knew if she didn't just accept his answer meekly, he would get ugly.

"Have fun then." Sarah—Spooky—Walters ended the call and set her cell phone on the counter. She wanted to just toss supper in the trash, but the baby needed to eat and so did she.

She wiped the tears from her eyes and sat down, forcing herself to eat the meal she'd prepared for him. When she'd had her fill, she threw the rest in the trash. She went into the living room and curled up on the couch with a romance novel. She'd heard many bad things about romances, but she had to get the feelings a romance brought up from somewhere, and she was getting nothing from Doug.

Thinking about how strangely her life had worked out, she plopped the book on her belly, and thought back over the last two years.

She and Doug had dated in high school, but when she'd gone off to college, he'd taken a job with a local mechanic. She hadn't dated much in college, always knowing she'd come back to her little town in Delaware and marry her high school sweetheart.

She'd done her degree in three years, and her masters in two. When she came home for the summer between her master's degree and doctorate, she'd happily reunited with her Doug.

Halfway through the summer, he'd begged her not to go back to school and stay home and marry him. She'd compromised by doing an online doctorate and marrying the month she was supposed to go back to school.

Everything had been good at first, but as soon as she'd gotten pregnant, Doug had become distant, telling her that she shouldn't have gotten herself knocked up so quickly.

It hadn't made sense to Spooky. She'd expected him to be thrilled when she told him about the baby, but he hadn't been. He'd started "going out with the guys" every night after work, and most Saturday nights as well. She sat home alone, doing her classes or reading, and trying her very best to be the housewife that June Cleaver had been.

She cooked, cleaned, mowed the lawn, and made sure his laundry was always done up perfectly. Fixing her hair before he'd come home from work had become automatic, as well as slipping out of bed before he woke up so she could apply makeup.

She still couldn't figure out how she'd made such a mess of her life.

Picking up her book, she began reading again, losing herself in the latest Caroline Lee historical Scottish romance. What else did she have to do?

When her phone rang at shortly after two, Sarah woke up from where she'd fallen asleep reading on the couch and gone into the kitchen to answer it. It was probably just Doug suggesting he spend the night at one of the guys' houses so he wouldn't disturb her. Why he never realized calling disturbed her, she'd never know.

The number wasn't one she recognized. "Hello?"

"Is this Sarah Walters?"

Hearing her maiden name made her feel good. She'd decided not to give up the name she'd earned her degrees with. Why would she? "This is." She knew it couldn't be someone who knew her because they'd called her Sarah and not Spooky. She'd earned the nickname as a young child who always talked to the "ghosties" in the house.

"Your husband has been taken to the hospital in an ambulance. He was in an accident. It doesn't look good, so I'd get there as fast as you can."

She stood still for a moment before whispering, "Thank you. I'm on my way."

Spooky grabbed her keys and rushed out the front door, getting into her car. It was the car she'd been given for graduating from high school. It had been used when she got it, but it still ran, and as she drove through the dark streets of town, she ignored the tears pouring down her cheeks, and stopped at the emergency room entrance to the hospital, knowing that was the only entrance that would be open in the middle of the night.

Hurrying through the door, she saw them bring Steve into the hospital. They were doing CPR on him as they moved him. Ignoring Doug's friend Steve she walked to the counter to the nurse who seemed to be triaging, though it seemed to be only the ambulance bringing people in. The hospital was eerily quiet at that time of night.

"Hello, I'm Sarah Walters. My husband Doug Ellickson was just brought in by ambulance."

The nurse nodded. "Let me take you to him."

As she followed the nurse, Spooky rubbed her unborn child, praying that the little tyke wouldn't grow up without his father. She hoped Doug was in better condition than Steve, and she couldn't help but wonder who had been driving drunk and caused a car accident like this.

As she walked into the room where Doug had doctors and nurses hurrying around him, she knew it was much worse than her mind had been able to conjure an image of. Equipment was beeping, and he was lying still.

No one noticed as she stood there, watching the hospital staff fight to save her husband's life. Finally, after a long while, the doctor who had been fighting so hard to save her husband shook his head. "Time of death four-nineteen."

Spooky stood for a moment with her hand over her mouth, incapable of saying a word. Her eyes were mysteriously dry as the staff left her with a few moments to say her goodbyes.

She held his hand there in the little room, wondering how so many people had fit, and finally she stood up straight. "Goodbye, Doug. You'll always be my first love."

Walking into the waiting room, she called her mother-in-law first, explaining what had happened. His mother was wailing into the phone, and still her eyes were dry. It was odd how she'd cried before she knew what was happening, but now that it was over, she felt numb in every fiber of her body.

After ending the call with her mother-in-law still screaming, she called her own mother, and as she explained what happened, the tears started. Big ugly cries that wouldn't let her catch her breath.

"I'll be at the hospital in a few," her mother promised.

When her mother arrived, Spooky just let her deal with everything while she sat back and observed, crying her heart out.

Finally, her mother drove Spooky home with her brother, with his newly minted drivers' license following behind in her car.

TWO WEEKS LATER, SPOOKY was still in a daze. She sat with her mother on her sofa, staring off into space. "What are you going to do?" her mother asked for the tenth time since Doug had died, along with his buddies Steve, Michael and Jonathan. The picture was clear in all of their minds what had happened.

The bar closed, and they'd all piled into Michael's car, believing he was the most sober of the bunch. They'd swerved into oncoming traffic and a semi had plowed into the car, hitting it head on. The semi driver had been apologetic, but he'd been stone cold sober. He just hadn't been able to anticipate them swerving into his lane.

"I don't know," Spooky finally said, answering her mother's question for the first time. "I want to finish my PhD, but I need to be able to support the baby. I suppose I could go back to the university and teach there as an undergrad, or I could find another husband." At that she laughed. What kind of man would marry a woman who was five and a half months pregnant with another man's son?

"I can't imagine being a new mother and going to school and teaching. It just won't work." Mom bit her lip and then said something that shocked her daughter. "Spooky, I read about a woman who is based in New York who matches people up at the altar. She'd be certain that the man would be accepting of a pregnant wife. I called her and talked to her about your situation."

Spooky stared at her mother for a moment. "Seriously? You think I should marry a stranger?"

"It's either that or move in with me and your brother." The way Mom said it, there was no doubt in Spooky's mind that was the last thing she wanted to happen. When Spooky had moved off to college, Mom and Jeremy had moved into a smaller apartment. There was no room for two more people.

"I guess I can talk to her," Spooky said, uncertain she even wanted to talk to the woman, but the alternatives weren't pretty.

"She'll be here at noon tomorrow to interview you," Mom said, a smile on her face.

"What if I'd said no?" Spooky asked, feeling a little more like herself than she had in a very long time.

"Then I'd have called with egg on my face, and begged her forgiveness."

"Where should I meet her?"

"She's coming here. Your house. She has oral tests she'll give you to make sure you're not deranged and will end up with the right man for you."

"Oh, Mom, it feels like I'm betraying Doug's memory!"

"Your husband went out drinking and left you home and pregnant on your first anniversary. You owe him nothing." Mom had never been a huge fan of Doug's but she'd kept her opinion mostly to herself. Apparently, the gloves were off.

After considering for a moment, Spooky nodded. Her marriage had been a disaster for months. "All right." Though the guilt was still in the back of her mind. Shouldn't she wait until he was cold in his grave before looking for a replacement for him?

At a few minutes before noon the following day, Spooky heard a loud crash from the driveway. She pulled the cookies she'd made out of the oven and peered out the front window. A woman with purple hair and a big smile got out of the car and looked between the telephone pole and her car's bumper, then shrugged and headed to the house.

How anyone could be so blasé about a car accident was a mystery to Spooky, but perhaps this woman hits things more often than most.

She opened the door before the woman could knock. "You're Spooky!" the purple haired woman announced with a huge smile. "Don't worry about your telephone pole. My bumper took most of the damage. I'm Dr. Lachele Simpson. May I come in?"

Spooky felt more than a little overwhelmed by the woman's outgoing personality. "Hello." She opened the door wide, welcoming her inside.

Dr. Lachele put both her hands on Spooky's belly. "It's a boy, isn't it?"

"Yes, it is. How can you tell?"

"Oh, a bit of fairy godmother magic...and your mother told me on the phone."

Spooky found herself smiling for the first time since the accident. "I baked some chocolate chip cookies. Would you like some?"

"That sounds wonderful. Do you have milk to go with them? I've never been able to figure out how someone could eat cookies without drinking milk. It's like a crime against humanity!"

Spooky felt the smile creeping back onto her face. It felt strange but good. "I have milk."

They spent the entire day just chatting and getting to know one another. It was after six when Spooky finally asked, "Don't we need to start the test?"

Dr. Lachele laughed. "It's already over. Let me take you out to supper. What's good around here?"

Spooky wasn't going to deny the woman. She was hungry and had been fretting about what to serve while they'd talked. "There's a little Chinese place where they make the best hot and sour soup. I could eat it for every meal."

"What are we waiting for?" Dr. Lachele asked, grabbing her purse. "I hope you don't mind riding with me."

"Umm...would you mind riding with me? I have a baby to keep safe."

"You're smart. I'm probably the worst driver on the entire east coast."

"Are you not worried you'll hurt someone?" Spooky asked.

"Oh, no. Not at all. I seem to only be a danger to stationary objects. Never to people." Dr. Lachele shrugged. "I do my best to be safe around humans."

"Well, that's good." Spooky wasn't sure if it really was though, so she drove to the restaurant.

"I'm assuming you'd like a man who is willing to take on another person's child?"

Spooky laughed, and the sound was foreign to her ears. "I think I'll need one because little Goblin here is going with me wherever I go."

"Goblin, eh?"

"When I was first pregnant, I felt like a goblin had taken over my insides. I've called him Goblin since day one."

"I like it!"

"My husband did not. He said I shouldn't be calling his kid a Goblin, though he seemed to think I got pregnant on my own, so I don't know why he called it his kid anyway."

Dr. Lachele covered Spooky's hand with hers. "It's okay if you don't worship the ground he walked on. He was a man, and he had faults. You don't have to act like he was perfect."

With those words, Spooky felt a bit of the weight fall off her shoulders. "I spent all day on our anniversary making a romantic supper for us to share. He called and said he was going out with his buddies. So I spent my anniversary home alone, and he died that night."

Dr. Lachele nodded. "I understand. You need a man who will treat you right."

"I do."

Chapter Two

Chase Appleby stood at the front of the church where generations of his family had been married, waiting for his mysterious bride to walk down the aisle toward him. The valley where he lived in Clover Creek, ID, had been settled by his family after they'd traveled the Oregon Trail.

Chase was as far removed from that journey as a twenty-first century man could be. His college sweetheart, whom he'd met in Pocatello at Idaho State University, had died shortly before graduation, and he simply didn't have the heart to look for another love.

So he'd followed the advice of a friend and contacted a matchmaker, who had found a woman, whom he would meet at the altar. It sounded crazy even as he thought it, but how much did it truly matter? He was going to marry, have someone to share his life with, and there would be another generation of Applebys to ranch on the hill overlooking the town of Clover Creek.

He was the only son of the Applebys who hadn't moved off and made their lives elsewhere. The area was cold with an average of 79 inches per year of snow, but it was home. Chase couldn't imagine living anywhere else.

He jumped when the music started playing, and all of his attention went to the beautiful blonde walking down the aisle toward him. She was accompanied by an older woman, he could only surmise was her mother. Her hands clutched a bouquet of flowers in front of her.

When she reached the front of the church and took his proffered hand, he leaned down and whispered, "Chase." He thought it would be best if his bride knew his name before they said, "I do."

"Spooky," she whispered back.

"Why is Chase a spooky name?" he asked, never having had that sort of reaction to his name before.

"My name is Spooky," she whispered, immediately straightening up when the pastor gave her a look.

Throughout the ceremony, he watched her. She still clutched the flowers in front of her with one hand, as if she was afraid to put them down.

Once they'd both spoken their vows, her flowers were taken from her, and his eyes widened in surprise. That's what she was hiding. A very pregnant belly. Well, he'd said he wouldn't mind an instafamily, and apparently, that was exactly what he was getting.

After the ceremony, he introduced her around, going to the church's Fellowship Hall to have a snack that had all been arranged by his father's housekeeper. His mother had died when he was small, and his father had never remarried, so Mrs. Turner had been the only real mother figure he'd ever had. It hadn't been decided yet whether she was staying with him, or moving to Arizona with his father. Either way, he knew they would be getting help for his pregnant wife.

When they finally had a moment where no one was speaking to them, he leaned down. "Where did you get the name Spooky? Pastor called you Sarah."

"When I was a little girl, I kept talking to the man who lived in my house. The man no one else could see. He once told me that there would be a fire, and everyone had to get out. Somehow I convinced my family to leave the house with me, and the flames were visible as soon as we got outside. I've been Spooky ever since."

He grinned. "It's a lovely name."

She laughed. "It's a silly name, but it's hard for me to remember to respond to Sarah, so if you'll just go with it, I'd appreciate it."

It wasn't until a few hours later when they were in his home—her new home—that they could really talk. There was plenty of food left from their reception for them to have for supper. "Are you sure you don't mind eating that again?" she asked. "I could whip something up."

"No need," he said, patting the spot on the couch beside him.

"Thank you. The journey was long. Is the closest airport really three hours away?" Spooky didn't think anyone in the US lived so far from civilization.

"There's one two-hours from here, but the prices tend to be twice as much. Most people just fly out of Salt Lake because it's easier."

"I see. So what part of Idaho are we in? Not that it will mean much to me because I've never been in Idaho and know nothing about the geography here."

"We're in the southeast corner of the state. We're about twenty minutes away from Wyoming, and thirty from Utah."

"I see."

"Where are you from, Spooky?" Chase felt silly calling her that, but if that's what everyone else called her, who was he to try to change her name?

"Delaware."

"And how did you end up pregnant, in Idaho, sitting on a couch with a virtual stranger who is also your husband?"

She took a deep breath before responding. "I married my high school sweetheart between graduate school and starting my doctorate in English literature. Doug was a wonderful husband until he found out I was pregnant. He started going out with 'the guys' more and more. On our first anniversary, he was out with the guys, and they had been drinking. The guy driving swerved into oncoming traffic where a semi hit them head on. I made it to the hospital right before Doug died. All four of them died actually. Semi was barely dented."

"I'm so sorry for your loss."

"Thank you," she said automatically. She'd had enough people say those words to her in the past six weeks that she hoped she'd never hear them again. "What about you? You're a good looking guy, and judging by this house, you're not hurting for money. Why did you go to Dr. Lachele?"

"My story is similar to yours. I found the girl of my dreams in college, and we were going to come back here, marry, and take over the ranch from my dad." Chase looked down at his hands. "Felicia was in a convenience store, looking for study snacks, and a guy walked in with a gun. He shot her and the guy behind the counter. She died instantly."

"Oh, that's horrible. Did they catch the guy?"

Chase nodded. "He's doing a life sentence with no possibility of parole." He shook his head. "I haven't really felt like dating or looking for anyone since. I just never felt like I could replace her. My dad has been on me to find a wife ever since, and finally, I just called Matchrimony. I didn't have the heart to find someone, fall in love, and marry. So I skipped a couple of steps."

"I understand completely. I've been working on my doctorate, and the idea of studying, working, and caring for a baby was way too much for me. I would have lost my mind and never known little Goblin."

Chase's lips twitched. "Goblin?"

"I've called him that since the morning sickness started. Only a goblin could make me feel so terrible."

"It's a boy?" he asked, liking the idea of having a son.

Spooky nodded. "Yes. And no, I don't have a name yet. We have two and a half months to figure that out. I had almost decided on a name, but when Doug died, everything changed for me."

"Do you want to name him after his father?"

She shook her head adamantly. "I really don't. I'd rather come up with a name that wouldn't remind me, if that makes sense."

"Absolutely. We'll order a baby book from Amazon and go through baby names together. Goblin works though."

Her eyes widened. "Please tell me you have a hospital close where I can give birth."

He grinned. "Come with me." She followed him to his back deck, and he pointed out over some trees. "Do you see that white roof?"

"Yes."

"That's where the helicopter lands when someone needs to be flown to a larger hospital. This one is good for simple surgeries and babies. I'm not saying the doctors here aren't good, because most are, but the hospital isn't equipped for anything major, like a heart surgery or something."

"Well, even in the dead of winter, I could get there!" She smiled. "That's one thing I won't have to worry about."

"Not at all." He moved back toward the couch, and she followed him. "So how do we want bedroom arrangements to be? There are plenty of spare rooms so you could move into one of those, or you could sleep with me. I had thought we'd sleep together, but if you want to wait til the baby is born..."

"I would prefer that, if you don't mind. I feel anything but sexy with this little boy going everywhere I go, but a foot in front of me. Or is it ten feet?" She looked down at her stomach and frowned.

"You're beautiful just like you are. You shouldn't worry about that at all, but I don't mind either way. I think it will be nice to have time for us to get to know one another."

"It will. You don't mind if I go ahead and continue my studies do you? I have a scholarship that pays for most of them." She bit her lip, hoping he wouldn't be like Doug and think she was silly for even wanting a PhD.

"Of course not! You had a life before me, and I have no problem with that. I should show you the bedrooms so you can choose the one you want for the baby."

He stood and led her to the stairs. "This house was originally built by Jacob Appleby, and the core of it is still his work. It's been added on to by different generations, and I think each one put its own touch on things. So up here are the original bedrooms, and there are four of them." He opened each door to a tiny bedroom with no bathroom, and she wasn't certain any would work. The baby loved to kick her bladder during the night.

"I get my pick of them?" she asked.

"No, I'm going to let you pick from the downstairs bedrooms."

"Oh, thank God!"

He chuckled. "I wouldn't want you to be uncomfortable."

Leading her back down the stairs, he took her to a bedroom with an adjoining bath. "The bathroom hooks you to the next room, which would be great for you to have one, and the other be a nursery. I think this one should be the nursery though."

She looked into the huge bedroom and smiled. "I don't think he needs anything half this big."

Chase shrugged. "But there will be room for toys. And hopefully siblings down the road."

Spooky nodded. This man certainly seemed to be a good one. She would love to have more children if there was support for her. "Sounds good."

He led her to the room next door, and opened the door wide. "This is the room I'd choose for you."

"Oh, my! This is like a bedroom and a sitting room all in one."

"What do you think?"

"I love it!"

"Good. Now we have rooms chosen for both you and Goblin." He nodded to the next door. "That's my room there. I'll be within yelling distance."

"Sounds good to me." The room they'd chosen for her was rather drab, and she'd love to spruce it up, but she wasn't going to spend any more than he gave her for grocery shopping.

"All right. I'm getting hungry. Let's eat some more of our wedding feast."

She laughed at that. There had only been about thirty people at the wedding, including her mother. She didn't know why there hadn't been more, and she wasn't about to ask him that yet. They'd only met a few hours before.

Going into the kitchen, she pulled out different foods from their reception and heated the ones that needed to be heated. She looked around at all the cabinets, wondering where she could find a plate. Finally she asked. "Plates?"

He shrugged. "No idea."

Spooky looked at him to see if he was joking, and the look on his face told her he was dead serious. "Why not?"

"Mrs. Turner always gave me my meal on a plate, and she did the dishes and put them away." Chase shrugged as if it wasn't at all odd not to know where the plates were in his own house.

"Mrs. Turner?"

"Housekeeper. She's been here since my mother died when I was two."

"Oh." Did that mean Mrs. Turner would stay on? She wasn't sure she liked the idea of someone living with them in their first few months of marriage.

"I think she's going to move to Arizona and keep working for Dad. I'm not sure yet, though. Part of that depends on you."

Spooky gave him an odd look. "I've never had a housekeeper. I wouldn't know what to do with one!"

He chuckled. "Off she goes to Arizona then. But in the meantime, we should probably search for plates."

Spooky started opening cabinets, and found the plates, putting out one for each of them. The kitchen was big with both a table and stools for the bar. She'd already seen the dining room with the huge table. It was hard for her to believe he'd grown up in a house like this with just his father and a housekeeper. There needed to be a large family living there and kids running around everywhere.

They filled the plates and moved to the table to eat. "I'm glad you didn't want to eat on the stools," she said. "I'm not sure I have the energy to climb that high tonight."

He grinned, covering her hand with his. "You're doing just great."

After a quick prayer, they ate their meals, and Spooky did her best not to stare at him. She wanted to stare because he was quite handsome. She couldn't believe she'd lucked out so well by marrying a stranger that an odd purple haired woman had chosen for her. Life was very strange.

As soon as they were done eating, she put the dishes in the dishwasher and ran it, putting what was left of their 'wedding feast' back into the refrigerator. She needed a hot bath, but she wasn't about to be rude and tell him she needed to take a bath and be alone.

They talked well into the night. It was just after midnight when he realized it was all she could do to keep her eyes open. "You need to go to bed!" Chase told her. "I didn't think about how tired you must be from your long day of travel."

"I do need to sleep," she said, smiling at him. "And I'm taking a long bath in the morning in that beautiful tub. So don't worry if I come out late."

"Fine by me. I'll be up early to get the men started on their work for the day."

"The men?" she asked.

"It takes about a hundred men to keep up a ranch of this size."

Spooky blinked a few times. "That sounds like a lot of work to keep up with a few cows."

He laughed. "Cattle, and it's not a few." He kissed her forehead. "Go to bed. I should be done with work by about noon, and then we'll figure out how we're going to do things."

"I have to do some schoolwork this week, but it can definitely be put off until Tuesday."

"Good. I need you to myself tomorrow."

Chapter Three

After her bath the following morning, Spooky went into the kitchen to warm up more of the leftovers from the day before, so they could have them for lunch. She'd slept much later than she'd expected. She didn't know if it was pregnancy, being on east coast time, or jet lag, but something had her dragging.

She'd barely made it to the kitchen before noon, and she hurried to get everything ready. While different dishes microwaved, she dug through the cabinets and refrigerator, noting they were pretty well stocked.

Spooky knew they were running out of leftovers, and soon it would be time for her to start cooking. She wasn't a great cook, but she was learning as she went along.

The last dish wasn't out of the microwave when Chase joined her. "I'm sorry! Lunch isn't quite ready."

"I was going to take you out to lunch. There's this great restaurant in Fish Haven, just before you get to the Utah border. I thought I'd show you around and feed you a delicious meal."

"I didn't know. I can put everything back." Spooky waited for him to get angry with her for not anticipating his needs as Doug always had.

"I'll help you put it back. I promise you'll enjoy this restaurant. We can't sit outside because it's snowing, but we should still have a good view of the lake."

"Lake?"

Chase grinned. "Bear Lake. I think it's the most beautiful lake in the world with the bluest waters."

"Well, we should go then."

"It's a big tourist area, and soon you'll be like the rest of us around here, cussing the extra traffic they cause. I feel like I live in the most beautiful place in the world though."

There was a knock at the door and an older man came in, a woman at his side. "Chase, we decided to leave earlier than planned. We're heading down to Arizona in a few hours."

Chase nodded. "Be careful going through the canyons. It's snowing."

His dad nodded. "I know. That's why we're leaving now. I'm not going to get stuck in another nine months of winter in Bear Lake because I'm afraid to drive the canyons with my truck."

"Are you pulling a trailer?" Chase asked.

"Yes. It's time for me to go. I'll be back every summer to live in the little house, but I'm not spending another blasted winter here."

Mr. Appleby's gaze drifted to Spooky. "When are you due?" he asked.

"January twelfth. I'm having a boy."

"And what happened to the boy's father?" Mr. Appleby sounded slightly accusatory, and for a moment, Spooky hesitated.

"He was killed in a car wreck six weeks ago. I didn't want to raise him alone, so I sought help."

"Well, that's just fine. I would like for you to call when he's born. I look forward to my first grandson. I hope you'll give me many more."

Chase put his arm around Spooky's waist to show his father she had his protection, and his father nodded approvingly. Then Chase turned his attention to Mrs. Turner. "I'm going to miss you."

Mrs. Turner's eyes filled with tears. "I'll miss you as well, but my place is with your father."

He walked to the older woman and encompassed her in his strong arms. "Thanks for being my second mom."

"I guess I should tell you we're marrying as soon as we get to Arizona. She's worked for me long enough. A wife is what I need now," Mr. Appleby said.

Chase grinned and held out his hand to shake his father's. "I'm glad. She's been my mother for years. It's time she was your wife."

The smile on his dad's face told him he'd said the right thing. "Well, we're going to go pack up the last of our things and get on the road."

"Which canyon are you taking? I'd almost go through Grace with that trailer and the snow."

Mr. Appleby nodded. "That's what I plan. I'm not going to take those tight turns with that trailer."

Spooky watched the whole thing. She realized then she really did have a lot in common with Chase. She'd been raised mostly by her mother, and he'd been raised mostly by his father. Life was strange.

She finished putting everything up and found her socks and shoes. Putting them on was becoming a bit of a chore, but she was strong, and she certainly wasn't going to ask for help. It was a matter of pride.

She grabbed her winter coat from her room, thankful she'd brought it. Her mother had suggested she ship it to her, but Spooky had a strong feeling that she'd need it before it could be shipped.

"I think I'm ready."

He looked her up and down and nodded. "You look great."

She laughed. "It's going to be a while before I look great." She patted her burgeoning belly, and he grinned.

"You can be pregnant and look great. And you do."

He kept a hand on her elbow as he guided her out to the car. "I've had feelers out for a housekeeper for us. I don't think you should feel the need to cook and clean when you're in a doctoral program."

"I don't need that. I can do it all. I promise!"

"I'm not going to ask you to." He opened the passenger door of his SUV and climbed in to drive. "This car is going to be yours to do errands and whatever else you need to do. I have a truck I use out on the range, so this will be available for you."

"I never thought about needing a car."

"Well, we mostly have to go get what we need. The nearest Walmart is an hour and a half away. So is the nearest McDonalds. We are very remote here, but we have our little town supporting us."

Spooky shook her head. "And everyone in town is just going to accept that you've found yourself a wife who is pregnant with another man's baby?"

He shrugged. "I don't care what they think. Besides, I'm already thinking of that baby as mine."

He started down the hill, pointing out the best way to go. "As soon as there's enough snow, they're going to block off that steep street. Then we'll have to go this slower way. It's smart though."

"I can see the sledding would be good around here."

Chase laughed. "Oh, trust me, it is. We're surrounded by mountains. Sledding, snowmobiling, four-wheeling, hiking, swimming, hunting. We're in an outdoor paradise. My ancestors arrived here in 1852, and my family has ranched the same land ever since."

"Oh, it must be so neat to live on land that your ancestors chose so long ago."

"It is." Chase had a smile on his face as he said the words. "To your left is the only grocery store in town. There are two main streets. The one we're on is Washington, the other is 4th Street or Highway 30. I'm taking Washington out of town and around the lake. I'll point out important things as we go."

"Sounds good."

After the intersection, he pointed to the left again. "Maverik. The place for snacks in the middle of the night. Past that is all of the doctors in a couple of buildings, and then you can see the hospital emergency room."

"The hospital is tiny!" Spooky wasn't sure if that should make her nervous.

He nodded. "It is. But remember they fly you out of here as soon as it's something they can't handle. Broken bones and babies are the specialty." Pointing left again, he said, "Middle school. To the right is city hall."

They continued that way until they crossed a big bridge and all she could see was countryside. "Not hard to see where the city ends, is it?"

He chuckled. "We're a small community. Clover Creek is only about twenty-five hundred people."

"It is definitely beautiful." Spooky had felt like she lived in a small town in Delaware, and there had been ten thousand people there. This town would definitely be an adjustment. "Does it always snow this early in the year?"

"I've seen it snow in September many times. It's not every year, but it's often enough no one thinks much of it. I've also seen it snow in June."

"That's crazy! I love snow, and even I think I'd be bored of it by June."

"Most of us are. But we still love our little valley." He pointed to the right. "If I went that way, it would take us to Emigration Canyon, which is the safer canyon in the winter."

"Is there a way out of town where we don't have to go through any canyon?"

He nodded. "Trust me. You get used to all this stuff."

By the time they got to the restaurant, she felt like she had an idea of what the community held in store. He stopped right in front of the restaurant to let her out. "Sorry, but I need to park up the hill a bit, and I don't want you slipping and falling."

"I appreciate it." Spooky opened the door and stood just inside the place. The snow had let up a little, and she could see the lake out of the far window.

"How many?" the hostess asked.

"Two. And can I request a table by the window? I want to see the lake better."

"Is this your first time?"

Spooky nodded. "Just moved into the valley yesterday."

"Oh, you'll love it here if you don't mind cold and snow."

"I'm from Delaware, so I'm used to cold and snow. Not usually this early in the year, but we get cold weather."

"So what brings you to Bear Lake?" the hostess asked.

"I married a man here." Spooky didn't want to tell the whole long story of losing her husband.

"Oh, a local?"

Spooky nodded. "Chase Appleby."

"Oh, he's hot. I went to high school with him. Well, we all went to high school together. And middle school. There are three elementary schools, but only one middle and one high school. So everyone knows everyone else in the valley."

"I can see where that would happen." Spooky heard the door open behind her. She turned to see Chase, and he gave her a smile that made her weak in the knees. The hostess was right. He really was hot.

"Hey, Chase. I didn't know you were getting married."

"It was a sudden thing," Chase said, and Spooky was glad she hadn't told the whole story. Chase seemed to think it should be kept quiet.

The hostess glanced at Spooky's belly but said nothing more. She led them across the restaurant to the windows overlooking the lake. Instead of sitting right down, Spooky went to the window and stared out over the lake. They were too far to see their house, but the lake was absolutely stunning.

"Tell me you have a boat, and are going to take me out on the lake this summer."

Chase walked up behind her and chuckled softly. "I sure do, and I sure will. We'll put the baby in a tiny life jacket."

The hostess put their menus on the table. "Your server will be with you shortly."

By the time their server asked for their drink orders, they were sitting at the table and perusing the menu. "You like sprite?" he asked.

She nodded. "Sure."

"Get us both a lime rickey."

"Sure, Chase. Any appetizer?"

He shook his head. "No thanks." Looking at Spooky, he said, "I don't care what you get to eat, but your side should be their sweet potato fries."

"That sounds good. I'll try them. Do you mind if I get a steak? Ever since I got pregnant, I've been craving red meat."

"Anything you want. I'm probably going to get the crab legs."

She frowned. "Are crab legs safe this far inland?" In Delaware, she'd always heard they were only safe on the coast.

"I've never had a problem here. There's a seafood place in Afton, Wyoming that's to die for."

"How far away is Afton?"

"Around fifty minutes from our house. We seriously are right on the border of Utah and Wyoming."

"There's no Walmart in Afton?"

He shook his head. "There's one in Pocatello which is an hour and a half north. One in Logan, Utah which is an hour and a half through one of two canyons. Those are the closest."

"Do you go often for supplies?"

He shrugged. "Once a month or so, if I feel like it. Usually, we shop here in town. There's a hardware store, a grocery store… We even have a redneck witchdoctor."

Spooky blinked a few times. "I'm not going to ask what that is if you don't mind."

"Nah. Totally fine." He grinned. "We even have a gun and liquor store."

"That doesn't sound like a good idea."

"Probably not. You never know what you'll see in there. They have a wide variety of stuff to buy. Lots of fishing equipment and outdoorsy stuff. This crazy guy runs it. I went to school with his kid. I have no idea what his real name is, but he wants everyone to call him Thor."

Their drinks came, and Spooky was surprised to see that a lime rickey was purple. She'd expected green. They placed their order, and she took a sip of the drink. "Oh, this is delicious."

"It's a regional drink, but my favorite. There's a little shed in town that's a soda shop kind of place. You can get gourmet coffees, but you can also get all kinds of blended drinks. They have the best lime rickeys."

"You're going to need to show me this place." Looking out over the lake, she couldn't help but smile. A lake with mountains and trees surrounding it. It really was an outdoor paradise as far as she was concerned.

Chapter Four

On their way home from the restaurant, Spooky told Chase, "You were so right about those sweet potato fries. The cinnamon and the marshmallow dipping sauce...I will now want them for every meal."

He laughed. "Of course you will. I'm glad you liked it. We'll go back."

"Other than red meat I'm craving Chinese food. Is there a Chinese place in town?"

Chase sighed. "No, but there's a decent one in Soda Springs, which is about thirty minutes away. They have the best hot and sour soup on the planet."

"Really? That's my favorite! Dr. Lachele and I went to my favorite place for hot and sour soup the day she interviewed me."

"She's an odd duck," he said. "Ran into my mailbox."

Spooky laughed. "She ran into my telephone pole."

"How does she have a driver's license?"

"No clue. I never saw hers if she did have one, though. Maybe she's driving around hitting things with no license." Spooky was certain that was the case.

"Oh, you're probably right. I think she did a good job with us though. I mean, we're still in the getting to know you stage, but I feel like things are going well between us."

She bit her lip. "Does it bother you that I'm pregnant?"

He shook his head adamantly. "Not at all. I've always wanted a houseful of kids. Being an only child was lonely."

"I have a younger brother, but he's eight years younger, so I was an only for a good long while."

"You've mentioned your mom and a brother. Dad?"

"Took off when my brother was born. Said it was too much tying him down. He never wanted visitation rights, so I haven't seen him again. Mom said the only good thing about him was he paid his child support on time every month."

"I can't imagine not having a dad to lean on," Chase said, shaking his head. "I hope you know I will never be that way. Even with Goblin. The moment we married, he became my son."

"Doug didn't want him." It was the first time Spooky had said the words out loud, and she immediately felt awful. "I'm sorry. I shouldn't have said that."

"Is it true?" Chase asked, frowning. He couldn't imagine not wanting his own child.

"Unfortunately. The only thing he had to say is I shouldn't call him Goblin."

"Then I'm glad we're together now. Goblin is going to be loved by both parents, not just his mother."

"I'm not even sure what to say to that. How can you just embrace the idea of being a father to another man's child?"

"If I adopted a child, I wouldn't love it any less. Why wouldn't I love the one my wife is carrying because it's not mine?" Chase asked logically.

"Oh, I don't know. I don't know why he didn't."

"It sounds like he was a very selfish man. Going out with friends when he could be home with you. I can't picture that." He shook his head. "Maybe age is the difference. How old was he?"

"Same age as me. Twenty-five when he died. Twenty-four when we married." Spooky looked over at him. "How old are you?"

"Thirty-two. My dad has been waiting for me to marry so he could officially retire and move away."

"But there's a place where he'll spend summers on your property?"

"Yes, there have been lots of cabins and houses over the years. There's one not much smaller than the big house where we live, and he's taken it as his own. The ranch foreman has another. The fourth burnt down. From what I understand, my great great something grandfather moved here with his daughter and three sons. He and his three sons all had a house on property. What they did was each got an adjoining piece of land, and they put the houses in the middle so they were all close."

"That's interesting. Do you have animals other than the cattle?"

"According to family lore, we once had chickens, goats, horses, hogs, and cattle we raised. We still breed horses, and we have the cattle, of course. And we keep chickens for their eggs, but if we want to eat a chicken, we tend to go to the grocery store."

"Are the cattle the descendants of the original ones?"

"Maybe a few are, but we've gone to trying to breed a leaner beef here. I raise mostly angus, and I know they didn't care much about lean beef in 1852."

"That's really interesting. Do you have family records of these things?" she asked, thinking she would enjoy learning more.

"I do! Almost all of my ancestors kept journals of the journey here on the trail, but most seemed to enjoy it enough they kept going after they arrived, and even taught their children to do the same. In the attic is a huge box full of journals. I tried to read them once, but some are faded, and they're all written out longhand. It's a chore to get through them all."

"Would you mind if I took a peek?" she asked. "I'm looking for a project for my thesis."

"I'll bring the box down for you. I don't want you climbing around in the attic in your condition."

When they arrived home, she was still full. "You okay with leftovers for supper again? I think one more time, and they'll be gone. Do I need to return dishes?"

"No, Mrs. Turner did all the cooking for our reception. She's an amazing lady. I'm so glad she and Dad are finally tying the knot." Chase held her arm as they walked up to the house, obviously still worried she'd slip on the slick ground.

It occurred to Spooky that Doug had never done anything like it, and she knew if he'd been around, and she was pregnant in the snow, he wouldn't have. He didn't have a gallant bone in his body. "It's good that you're excited. Did you know they had feelings for each other?"

"I had a feeling. She was a friend of my mom's who lost her husband around the same time Mom died. So they banded together to raise me. She said her only regret was that she'd never had a child of her own, but I made up for it."

"I want to see the ranch sometime when it's a little less snowy," she said as she removed her coat and carried it into her room. "My things should be arriving in a few days, and I am going to have a lot of work to do just getting everything put up." She raised her voice so he could hear her, but saw that he was standing in the doorway. "I have one little outfit for Goblin. I found it on sale for seventy-four cents." She remembered the fight that had ensued when Doug had seen it. He hadn't thought she should be wasting money on clothes for the baby when there were other things they needed more.

"You've only bought one outfit? You're going to have to go to Bear Necessities. Our redneck witchdoctor has a boutique set up filled with baby clothes. I don't think there's quite as much for boys as for girls, but you'll still find a nice selection."

"Is that the only place to buy baby clothes in town?" she asked.

"Of course," he said with a grin. "You're probably going to want to order from Amazon or make the drive into one of the bigger cities to pick out furniture for the nursery and clothes for Goblin. And diapers. I mean, you can get them at our grocery store, but the prices are through the roof."

"I'll start ordering then," she said with a smile. "If you don't mind that is. I don't have much money of my own. I was barely able to cover funeral expenses."

He pulled his wallet out and handed her a credit card. "Limit on that is fifty-thousand. Let me know if you need more than that."

She choked. "I shouldn't need a fraction of that!"

"Don't skimp. Get Goblin what he needs."

She nodded, staring at the card in her hand. She had obviously underestimated what he made as a rancher. "Thank you."

He walked further into her room and wrapped his arms around her. "Only the best for our Goblin."

Spooky chuckled. "You just like saying Goblin."

"I really do. Not sure why..."

She laughed. His arms around her felt right. She'd expected it to feel strange because she'd only ever been with Doug.

"I was thinking about doing Mickey and Minnie Mouse for a theme for the nursery. What do you think?"

"Sounds fine to me. If you want to paint it let me know, and I'll get someone to do it for you. You don't need to spend that much time on your feet."

"I guess not." She felt a little let down. She'd been planning to paint the nursery herself. Not that she'd ever painted a room before, but she liked the idea of doing things for little Goblin. "I should probably get a doctor. Is there an OB in town?"

"There is, but I think all the doctors deliver babies. We're a family-focused community."

"I'll search for doctors on my phone then. I'm going to be happy when my desktop computer gets here. It's hard to do everything on my phone and iPad."

Chase led her across the hall and opened a door. "Feel free to use mine," he said, stepping back so she could see into his office.

"You really don't mind?"

"Not at all. And when yours gets here, we'll add a second desk so we can both work when we need to. What do you want to do with your degree?"

"I was planning to teach at the college level, but I may have to settle for online teaching or doing something else entirely. I do want to finish, though." Spooky and Doug had planned to move to wherever she found a job after she had her degree. As a mechanic, he could work most places. That wouldn't work with Chase though.

"That would be difficult, but I don't think it's impossible. If you add education in, you could teach here in town, or teaching online would be good if you cared to do that. You may want to focus on the kids for a few years before going back to work as well."

"That wouldn't bother you?" Spooky asked. She'd thought he would be like Doug and want her to get a job as soon as she could, so he wouldn't have to work so hard.

"Not at all. I think we make sure the kids are comfortable and in school, and then you can find a job if you want, or not if that's your choice. I think you should be able to choose what you want to do. We don't need you to work, or even finish your doctorate unless you just want to."

"I do want to finish my doctorate. I'll decide about working after that. I still have at least another year or two to go, especially with slowing down when Goblin is born, and even I don't think I can keep going to school full time with a baby."

"Good. I like that you're being realistic." He glanced at the time on his phone. "I'm going to see how the men are doing with moving the cattle closer to home, and I'll be home in a couple of hours. Is that all right?"

She nodded. "I'll get a doctor's appointment made, and then I'll probably nap for a bit. I'm not dealing with the time change as well as I had hoped."

Chase leaned down and pressed his lips against Spooky's forehead. "I'll be back soon."

As Spooky watched him leave, she was struck by what a good man she'd married. She needed to call Dr. Lachele and tell her what a great job she'd done.

She used his computer, finding the only female doctor in town and calling her. She knew she'd feel more comfortable with a female than the male OB anyway.

After calling the office, she added the date and time of her appointment to her phone calendar, and then pushed back. It felt strange being in the house alone, but good. She was very comfortable there.

She went straight back to bed and climbed back in, even though she'd already made it. She could always make it again.

She woke as she heard the front door open and bounced out of bed as quickly as a woman in her stage of pregnancy could. She rushed into the hallway to find him about to enter his room. "I'm sorry. I fell asleep."

"What are you sorry for?" Chase asked. "You're allowed to sleep anytime you want to."

"I just know it's better if I'm awake when you're home."

"Why?"

Spooky shrugged. "Because you deserve all my attention after a hard day of work."

He sighed. "I'm not your first husband, Spooky. I don't know what he expected of you but all I expect is that you take care of yourself and that baby. Oh, and I need you to interview some housekeepers on Friday morning. I have four women coming at eight, ten, twelve, and two."

She nodded. "I'll do my best."

"That's the thing though. You don't always have to do your best. Just be you."

"I made that appointment with the doctor," she said, following him into his room and sitting on the bed.

He grabbed a clean shirt from his drawer and pulled off the one he was wearing. It looked wet and had mud stains on it. She watched as he changed, and felt her heart beat a little faster at the sight of his bare torso. Her fingers tingled as she ached to touch him.

"I'll go while you change," she said, getting to her feet.

"No need. I'm done." He walked to the bed and sat down beside her. "I know it's awkward right now, but I want us to get close to one another. We can't do that if you're constantly running off."

She nodded. "I guess not."

"I want us to be able to have a real marriage once you're healed from childbirth. I won't ask for more before that, because I just don't know anything about pregnancies, and I imagine it would be weird. But as soon as the doctor clears you, you'll have to move in here with me."

"Is that so?" she asked, wanting more from him.

Chase nodded, leaning toward her and brushing his lips against hers lightly. It was she who deepened the kiss, opening her mouth and wrapping her arms around him.

Spooky sighed happily. Kissing him was everything she'd expected it to be. Passionate yet sweet at the same time. "I can still taste the marshmallow dipping sauce," she said, grinning up at him.

He laughed. "I hope you liked it just as much the second time."

"How could I not?"

Chapter Five

Spooky found a housekeeper she liked on Friday, and she promised to start work on Monday. She was a widow with three school-aged children. It felt strange to ask someone else to cook and clean for her, but she was relieved. The house was much bigger than her home in Delaware, and she wasn't sure she was up to taking care of it and having a newborn around the house.

When Chase came in from work that afternoon she told him all about it. "I hired someone today. Her name is Claire Jensen. She's going to start on Monday. I really like her, so I hope she works out. She'll need to leave around three every day, but she said she would cook and leave dinner in the oven warming."

"That sounds great. Her husband Mike was a good friend of mine. Great guy. We were on the football team together." He went into his room with her following along behind him.

As he stripped off his shirt and put on another, he asked, "Have you made dinner?"

"With how busy I was with the interviews today, I never even thought of it. I'm so sorry!"

"Stop saying that!" He told her. "I was hoping you hadn't started anything because I want Chinese for supper. Would you like some hot and sour soup?"

"Can we get some to bring back with us? Would be a great lunch tomorrow too!"

He grinned. "Yes, we can get some. I can get you two or three extra bowls of it if you'd like. The woman running the place is amazing. She owns it, cooks and serves there, all while raising a daughter alone."

"That is amazing. I can't wait to meet her."

"You'll love her as much as I do." He pulled a clean shirt over his head. "Get your shoes on and we'll go."

She frowned. "There's something else I have to do first."

Chase frowned at her. "What's that?" He'd gotten used to how she finished all she wanted to do for a day and spent all the time he was home with him. He'd told her it wasn't important to him, and he was realizing that it was very important.

She stood up and walked to him, wrapping her arms around him. "I forgot to kiss you hello."

A slow grin spread across his face. "Well, we certainly can't have that."

She kissed him with increasing passion. When she broke the kiss off, his eyes looked sleepy, and she was aware hers did as well. "We should do that more often."

"I don't know. I'm afraid my toes are going to fall off with all the cold showers I'm taking."

She frowned. "Should I back off? Or...we don't have to wait if you don't want to."

He thought about it for a moment but shook his head. As much as he was looking forward to Goblin's birth, he couldn't feel like she was really his while she was pregnant with another man's child. He knew his thinking was twisted, and he looked forward to after the baby was born. He was definitely starting to lust after his pretty little wife. "No, we said we'd wait, and we will."

"Are you sure?"

He nodded. "When we make love for the first time, it's going to be special."

"And it wouldn't be with me looking like this. I understand."

He took her hand and pressed it to the front of his jeans. "Trust me, it's not that."

She could definitely feel what he meant, squeezing a little through the denim.

He groaned and removed her hand. "Stop that!"

She shrugged, trying to hide the grin that was threatening to pop through. "It was *your* idea."

"Go get your shoes on, and we'll have Chinese. She has these crab wontons that are to die for."

"I could try those. Oh, I want to eat everything." Spooky hurried into her room and put her socks and shoes on, aware that he was right behind her. "You know, I like the hungry phase of pregnancy a lot more than I liked the sick to my stomach phase."

"I'm not sorry I missed that part." But he was sorry that she'd gone through it mostly alone. He wanted to strangle Doug sometimes, but he tried not to say anything negative about her late husband.

Once her shoes were tied, she stood and grabbed her coat. "Let's go!"

He was again super careful with her as she walked toward the SUV. She shook her head. "How do you think I'm going to shovel the driveway without you standing there making sure I don't fall?"

"Shovel the driveway? I'll be doing the shoveling. Why would I ask you to do it?"

She was silent for a moment, and just got into the car. Did most women not have the job of shoveling?

When he got in beside her, he took her hand. "You're not going to be shoveling the driveway. If you use a shovel, it will be to plant things, and only if you like to do that sort of thing. Mrs. Turner always planted a garden, but you do what you want."

She frowned. "You worry about me a lot more than Doug ever did. I always got up early after it snowed so I could shovel the driveway before I made his breakfast."

"When you tell me things like that, it really makes me angry for you. You're married, and I will be doing any shoveling. I actually use a four-wheeler to do the driveway, but I shovel the back deck."

"I'm sorry it makes you mad. It never really bothered me."

"Would he have expected you to do it while you were pregnant?"

She shrugged. "I think he would have. We never discussed it, but he made it clear that I would still need to take care of my normal household chores whether I was pregnant or not."

Chase sighed. "All right. No more complaining about him. Let's eat Chinese!"

"I want to try those wontons you mentioned. And if the hot and sour soup is as good as you say it is, I want a vat of it to swim in."

"I'm not so sure about a vat," he said, shaking his head. "Maybe a few bowls, so we can take some home though."

The drive took about thirty minutes to the nearby town of Soda Springs. He pointed things out along the way as he always did when they were out. When he pointed out the soda shop, she promised herself she'd go there and get another lime rickey. The taste of that drink lingered with her, and she wanted to try it again to see if it really was as good as she remembered.

The town of Soda Springs wasn't much bigger than Clover Creek, but they had a few more restaurants. She looked at the beat up old building he parked in front of, and she wanted to ask if he was serious, but instead she decided to trust him. He knew the area much better than she did after all.

He took her arm as they went inside to be greeted by a cheerful woman with a thick Chinese accent. "Good to see you!" she called.

Chase walked straight to a booth and sat down, watching to make sure she could slide in easily with her stomach, but she had no problem. He sat across from her, and just by inhaling, she knew she was in for a real treat.

When the waitress came over, she greeted Chase happily. "You never bring your girl to me before. She not like Chinese food?"

Spooky smiled. "She loves Chinese food. Especially hot and sour soup."

The waitress smiled. "I put in extra egg for protein for baby."

"Spooky is my new wife."

"It is so good to meet you." The words came slowly as she was obviously not as comfortable with English as she would have liked. "You want hot and sour soup and crab wontons? And a Coke?"

Chase nodded. "You never forget an order!"

"What would you like to drink?" she asked Spooky.

"Root beer." Spooky tried to be careful with how many soft drinks she had for Goblin's sake, but she'd been craving a root beer for a few days. She really needed to make it to the grocery store so she could stock up on some of her cravings.

As the waitress hurried to the kitchen, Spooky grinned at Chase. "I love her."

"It's impossible not to. And next time, she'll remember your order the same as she remembers mine."

"She's exceptional."

"She really is." He took a sip of his drink. "Do you really think you'll be happy with Claire? Her kids being in school won't be a hindrance?"

"Not at all. Her oldest is twelve, and she said if she ever needs to come back, she can leave the other two with her. I really love how flexible she is." Spooky leaned back. "And I see Dr. Miller Monday at ten."

Chase wanted desperately to be part of that appointment. He didn't know why he felt so connected to the baby, but he did, and he wanted to be there. "Do you mind if I go with you?"

She blinked a couple of times in surprise. "You want to?" Doug hadn't gone to any appointments with her. Not even the one to see if the baby was a boy or girl.

"Of course I do! If they do a sonogram, I want to see Goblin."

Spooky smiled. "Then, yes, of course you can come. But if they are doing anything where I have to get partially naked, I'd rather you stood by my head."

"Do they do that in these appointments?" he asked.

"Yes, sometimes. And I think with this being my first visit with Dr. Miller they might."

"Then I'll respect your privacy if it comes to that."

"I know we're married, and I'm being weird, but..."

Chase shook his head. "Say nothing else. I'll do what I can to help."

"I really appreciate it."

The wontons arrived then, and she immediately reached for one, dipping it in sweet and sour sauce. "Oh, this is delicious."

He nodded. "I kind of hate to share. Maybe I'll ask for another plate of them."

Spooky laughed. "If you want. I can just eat the one, though."

"No, we'll get another plate. I sure hope you love the soup as much as I do."

While they ate, he asked if she'd ordered anything for the nursery.

"There's a resale store in town. I saw it on the web. I think I'll go there and look for the big stuff first."

"No," he said simply, taking a sip of his drink through the straw.

"Why not?"

"Because this is my first child, and we're not cutting corners. I want a new crib and one of those things you change babies on. And they should match. And you want Mickey and Minnie. The wife of a friend of mine loves to paint, so I'll get her to come up and paint the walls if you want them done. Are you thinking blue?"

She nodded. "A pale blue. And there are some huge character accents for walls I will order if you're really okay with it."

"Of course, I am. The hardware store will mix any color for you, so we don't have to leave town for that. Order what you want from Amazon, and then we'll make a trip to Pocatello for diapers and stuff. I have a Costco membership, so we'll do Walmart or Costco or whatever else you want. There's a mall there, but I don't know what stores the mall has."

"Costco and or Walmart will be more than enough. I love the idea of shopping for the baby. I may order from Baby Gap or something online as well. They have such cute things." Spooky smiled. Before last week, she'd never thought she'd have the funds to get what she wanted for the baby. And here she was with a credit card she couldn't dream of maxing out for her little Goblin. "Do you want to look at things and help me decide?"

Chase shook his head, making a face. "Absolutely not. I have no interest at all in shopping for anything."

"But you'll take me to Walmart and Costco?"

"Sure. That's not the same. That's spending time with you, but not sharing an opinion with you about what we should get. See the difference?"

"Not really, but if that's better for you, I'm not about to complain." Spooky looked up as the waitress reappeared with two bowls of steaming soup. "We're going to need another plate of wontons too. He doesn't want to share."

The waitress gave Chase a look. "You need to share with your pregnant wife. I know you can share."

"I did share. And now I'll share another plate of them with her."

She shook her head. "I come back with more."

Spooky reached out and took his hand. "You make me smile."

Chase brought her fingers to his lips. "And you do the same for me. I can't complain."

She tried the soup and sighed. "It's perfect. And the extra egg makes it so much better."

He looked at her bowl. "Maybe I should stuff a pillow under my shirt next time, and I can get extra egg in mine."

"Maybe you should just let me be the one who is pregnant for a while." She shook her head at him. "I can see I'll be fighting you for my fair share of food for the rest of my life."

"As long as you're with me for the rest of mine, I don't care how much you fight for food."

On the drive home, she patted her belly. "Thanks for ordering me the extra soups."

"Hey, just remember two of the four are mine."

"But Goblin is hungry!"

"I don't know what I'm going to do with you."

"I have some ideas, but apparently they're going to wait until Goblin is born." Spooky grinned at him.

He groaned. "You are truly going to be the death of me. I've known you for less than a week, and I know I'll never recover."

Spooky couldn't believe how happy she was with Chase. Her opinions about marriage had gone downhill quickly once she was married to Doug. Now they were reversing. He was a good man and already cared about her. Everything about her life was different, and the changes were good. She almost felt bad for how quickly she was falling for Chase, but he was the antithesis of her first husband. Finally, she'd found a man who treated her as if she was special and important. Who could ask for more?

Chapter Six

Chase and Spooky kept to their promise to not do more than kiss before the baby was born, but each night their time on the couch together became more passionate. They found a show they both enjoyed that they binged together, but often she would look over to find him watching her or vice versa, and they would find themselves quickly locked in a passionate embrace.

At the doctor on Monday, Chase kept his promise to stay beside her head and not embarrass her. Dr. Miller did a sonogram so she could have her own knowledge of the baby. "You're measuring about twenty-seven weeks. Does that sound right?"

"It does."

Chase's eyes were glued to the monitor. "I can't see Goblin," he told the doctor.

"Goblin?" Dr. Miller didn't look much over twelve herself, but she had three small children at home.

"At first, he felt like a goblin inside me, and now I'm gobbling up everything in sight," Spooky said, grinning.

"Oh, I know just what you mean. I was the same way with all three of mine."

Chase sighed. "I want to see him."

"Oh, sorry," Dr. Miller said with a smile. She stood between the monitor and Spooky. "Here's his head."

As she pointed everything out, Chase nodded. "Thanks, Dr. Miller. Spooky and I are really excited."

Dr. Miller frowned. "Spooky? I have your name as Sarah."

Spooky laughed. "I've been known as Spooky my whole life. I used to talk to a man who wasn't there, and he told me to get out of the house when there was a fire when I was small."

"Was there a fire?" Dr. Miller asked.

"Yes, there was. The house burned down, starting in the hallway outside my room. Without Mr. Goober, I would have died."

"Interesting. I can see where that would earn you the nickname Spooky."

"I even have my name as Sarah 'Spooky' Walters on all my diplomas."

Dr. Miller wiped off the machine. "I really like that. I'll try to remember. It seems fitting that Spooky would give birth to Goblin as well." She looked over at Chase. "I'm going to need a family health history for your family, so we know what could crop up in the future for the baby."

Chase shook his head. "No. I'm not the biological father, just the dad who will raise him."

Dr. Miller didn't question what he said, instead looking at Spooky. "Can you get me a health history for his biological father's family?"

Spooky nodded. "I'll call his mother this afternoon. Can I bring it with me next time I see you?"

"Oh, of course. I don't need to see you for another month, but then we'll go to every two weeks. You're getting close."

"I was really relieved to find out there's a hospital in town." Spooky sat up, making sure the sheet still covered her legs.

"As long as there are no complications, everything can be done right here in town." Dr. Miller looked down at her computer. "Make an appointment for four weeks with the front desk as you leave. Do you have anything else you want to discuss?"

Spooky shook her head. "I'm good. Chase?"

"Am I allowed to be part of the delivery?" he asked.

"You're the father. As long as your wife doesn't mind, you can even cut the cord."

Chase looked at Spooky. "We'll talk about it."

After the appointment, Chase suggested they go to lunch at Ranch Hand. "It's a truck stop, but they serve breakfast all day, and the food is good."

"You know what? Claire is working all day today, and I'm not even there. Should we get something to take home?" Spooky wasn't worried about the integrity of the other woman, but she knew there were things she should be talking to her about.

"If you want. We could do Subway or Arctic Circle? Or I could get pizza?"

"A burger sounds really good. Still needing that red meat."

"I'll drop you off at home and go get you the best burger in town," he said.

The ground was perfectly dry, and he allowed Spooky to walk to the door on her own. Strangely enough, it felt odd to go to the door without him. Once in the house, she hung her coat in the coat closet and went to the kitchen, finding Claire on her hands and knees scrubbing the floor.

"How are things going?" Spooky asked.

"Good! How was the appointment?"

"Everything looks good. Goblin is measuring right for his age. We got to see him on the sonogram. I'm going to start ordering stuff for the nursery this afternoon. I'm getting excited."

Claire smiled, climbing to her feet. "I remember doing the nursery for my oldest. We used the same for all three, but the excitement was there with the first. Are you doing a theme?"

"Mickey and Minnie. Then if I have a girl next, I can keep the same nursery."

"Are you hungry? Could I fix you some lunch?" Claire asked.

"Chase is getting me the best burger in town."

"Dan's," Claire said. "They are so good!"

"Can't wait to try them then." Spooky walked over to sit at the table. "It's strange how just a doctor's appointment can wipe me out these days. I don't think I'm on Mountain Time yet."

"It won't take too horribly long. Have you gotten the candy for Halloween yet?"

Spooky shook her head. "No, I figure I'll hit the grocery store the day of. No big deal."

Claire's eyes widened. "This street is known for having the best candy in town. You're going to get around five-hundred kids, and they'll all expect full or king size candy bars."

Spooky shook her head. "Why has no one told me that?"

"I just did! Do you want me to just handle it? I would probably just order from Costco."

"No, I can order. I need to order nursery stuff anyway. I think I'm going to order a few cases of diapers in different sizes for Goblin."

"Have you thought about real names yet?" Claire asked.

"No, but Chase ordered a baby name book that will be here tonight. We'll start talking names then."

The door opened and she turned to see Chase come in with three white paper bags. "I need to go back out for the shakes," he said.

"Shakes? You're killing me. Do you know how big I'll be by the time this baby is born?"

"There'll just be more of you to love!" he called over his shoulder after dropping the bags on the counter.

"I'm not sure what to do with that man," Spooky said, shaking her head.

Claire grinned. "I can give you some pointers if you need them!"

"I think I'm all right for now." Spooky yawned. "I'm going to have to order quickly because nap time is right around the corner for me."

"You need to sleep now while you can. After the baby is born your sleep will never be the same again."

"That's what people keep telling me."

Chase hurried back in with three shakes. "I hope you haven't eaten, Claire. I got you a bacon cheeseburger from Dan's."

"Even if I wasn't hungry, I'd eat that bacon cheeseburger." Claire carried the bags to the table and got out three plates. "Thanks for including me, Chase."

"No problem."

"I thought I'd make lasagna and garlic bread for your supper. You'll need to pop both in the oven, but other than that, it'll be ready for you," Claire told him.

"Sounds good to me," Chase said. "No one ever makes me homemade lasagna."

Claire just rolled her eyes. "I happen to know that Mrs. Turner made you anything you wanted whenever you wanted. Don't try that with me." She sat down at the table and dug into the bags. "Oh, do you want me to eat alone? I never thought of that."

"Not at all," Spooky said. "As long as you're here, you're one of the family."

"I figured you'd feel that way, but I wanted to make sure."

Spooky reached for one of the shakes. "What kind did you get?"

"Chocolate," Chase responded. "What else would I get my pregnant wife?"

"Nothing if you know what's good for you," Spooky told him, marveling at the fact she could already joke with him in a way she'd never been able to joke with Doug.

While they ate, Claire talked about how her children were doing in school. "It's strange that Maggie is already in middle school. She loves it."

"You have great kids. Always have," Chase said.

"I can't wait to meet them," Spooky replied. It was odd listening to the other two, who had known each other a very long time. She felt a bit jealous, knowing they had a history between them.

"Oh, Aunt Stephanie said to come over Saturday night. She's having a family thing and wants us all there."

Spooky swallowed her bite of the best burger she'd ever eaten. "Are you two related?" she asked.

"Oh, yeah," Claire said. "We're cousins. I thought you knew?"

"It never occurred to me."

"Oh, we're all related somehow. The families who have been here for generations, I mean. We just don't even think about it, but we do make sure we're not too closely related to marry," Chase said.

Spooky felt like an idiot for the jealousy she'd felt. She didn't know what was wrong with her that she'd jumped to conclusions. Why would Chase have contacted Dr. Lachele if he was in love with Claire anyway?

After lunch, Chase headed out to work while Spooky went into the office to start ordering for the nursery. At three, Claire stuck her head in the room. "Lasagna is in the fridge. Stick it in the oven about five, and then throw the garlic bread in about five fifty. Everything will be done at six. And I'm off to get my kiddos."

"Thank you for everything today!"

"Of course. I'm just thrilled to have a job that works around my schedule. I'll see you in the morning."

As Claire left, Spooky pushed checkout on her Amazon cart, trying not to cringe at the price. It felt very strange spending someone else's money on her baby.

Then she crawled into bed, setting an alarm for five, so she could stick their supper in the oven. She still had to place her Costco order for the mountain of candy bars that would apparently be needed for Halloween night, but she'd do that while supper cooked.

When the alarm went off, she grumbled under her breath but got up to cook the lasagna. She was surprised at how little she was doing, but how tired she was as she did it. The baby was taking more out of her than she'd realized.

She sat back down at his computer, starting the Costco order. There were so many things she wanted to get as well as the candy bars. She ordered some wipes and diapers from Costco. It wouldn't be long before they were going through diapers like crazy.

When the doorbell rang, she jumped. She didn't know anyone in town yet, and it felt odd to go to the door. Just as she got there, the UPS truck pulled away, and she could see an entire mountain of boxes on the driveway.

All of her things had finally arrived from Delaware. Now she could wear more than the seven outfits she'd packed.

She started the job of carrying the boxes inside, putting them in the living room. They would go throughout the house, and it would take her a week to get everything unpacked and put away.

She was half through carrying the boxes in when the door opened. Chase stood glaring at her. "What do you think you're doing?"

Spooky frowned at him. "I'm bringing in all my things that just arrived from Delaware."

"You sit down. I can't believe you carried so much! You're going to hurt yourself and the baby."

Spooky sighed. "You know I'm pregnant not sick, right?"

"I do... But you need help. Wait til I have everything inside."

While he went out to bring in more boxes, Spooky went into the kitchen and put the garlic bread in the oven, and then she set the table. When Chase didn't see her in the living room, he went looking for her.

"You're supposed to be sitting!"

"I'm getting supper on the table. It'll be done in ten."

"Why can't you stay where I put you?" he asked, obviously exasperated.

"Because I'm not a toy! And I'm not broken. You heard the doctor. I'm perfectly healthy and so is the baby."

Chase shook his head. "And I want to keep it that way!"

She rolled her eyes. "And that means I have to sit around like a lump? Are you going to unpack all my boxes for me and find places for everything in them?"

He narrowed his eyes. "No, I'm not. Claire is. I'll pay her extra."

"I can do it! I don't want anyone else going through my things." Spooky didn't know where this man got off thinking he was in charge of her.

"You're just going to have to deal with it," he said. The oven beeped and she immediately went to get the food out. "Where are you going now?"

"I'm not letting our supper burn. You're insane." She put on an oven mitt and pulled the food from the appliance, carrying the lasagna over and putting it on a trivet and putting the cheesy garlic bread into a basket. "What do you want to drink?"

He shook his head. "I'm going to change out of this dirty shirt, and I'll bring in the rest of the boxes after supper."

"You'll allow me to do dishes, won't you?" she asked.

"No! We have a housekeeper for that."

"But she has to spend the whole day unpacking boxes while I watch her. How will she have time to wash the dishes?" Spooky had reveled in his attention at first, but now he was taking things too far.

He went into his room and shut the door behind him. It was the first time she hadn't gone in while he changed at the end of the day, and she was glad not to be invited. If he was going to be insane, then she would just ignore him.

She put drinks on the table and sat down, serving them each a piece of lasagna and adding garlic bread to their plates. When he came out to join her, he sat down and prayed. "Heavenly Father, please keep my wife from being so pigheaded that she hurts our Goblin. Thank you for this food. In Jesus's name. Amen."

Spooky stared at him for a moment. "I have no idea what has gotten into you."

"I don't like seeing you carry heavy things. It can't be good for the baby."

"Did you hear Dr. Miller tell me not to lift things? Did you hear her say I should sit and let everyone around me do everything?"

"Well, no."

"A pregnant woman should keep doing everything she's already been doing. Nothing new, but I did so much more than this before I was pregnant. So stop being a pain in my butt."

He glared at her, and they ate their meal in silence. It was their first fight, and he didn't like it one bit.

Chapter Seven

After supper, while Chase carried boxes inside, Spooky did the dishes and wiped off the table. It was just a matter of putting them into the empty dishwasher, so she didn't feel like it was too much work, and while she knew Chase would be angry, he already was. What difference did it make if she did what she knew she should?

Once all the boxes were in, he stood with his arms crossed watching her as she finished the task she'd set for herself. "We'd get along a lot better if you'd just let me take care of you," he finally said.

"I was taught that being married meant I took care of my husband. You don't allow that, so why should I allow you to take care of me?"

He sighed. "Why don't we just say that being married means we're taking care of each other?"

Spooky thought about it for a moment. "I kind of like that," she finally said.

"I do too." He moved to her side, pulling her into his arms. "I know we're just getting to know one another still, but to me you'll always be fragile because I met you when you were expecting."

"I'm anything but fragile," she said softly.

"I don't know if I can ever make myself see you any other way."

She sighed. "I don't want us to fight."

"I don't either. I think we've started out well."

She nodded. "I hate that we fought tonight."

He took her hand and walked to the couch with her, pulling her down onto his lap. "I think from now one, we're always going to sit like this."

She laughed. "I'm too heavy. I'll crush you."

"Please." He shook his head. "You barely weigh anything at all."

"You have me confused with someone else." She rested against him. "I kind of like it here though."

He kissed her. "I do too. I think I'm keeping you."

"You'd better be. Goblin and I would be lost without you." It struck her she hadn't felt lost when Doug had passed. She'd been sad, but she'd known that he wasn't really someone she could rely on anyway.

He put his hand onto her belly, touching it directly for the first time. "Does Goblin kick?"

She laughed, nodding. "All the time. If you press against my tummy a little more, he'll kick you. He hates anything pressing against him."

"Really?"

Spooky nodded. "Yeah, really. I'm surprised he wasn't acting crazy during his sonogram today. The last one I had, he positioned himself so he could kick the little wand they used as soon as they pressed it into me. I think we're going to find we have a boy who knows what he wants."

Chase pressed his hand a little harder into her stomach, and sure enough the baby moved and kicked his hand. "That's cool!"

She nodded. "The first time it happened it was sort of scary, but you get used to it. He likes to move around at night best, which is how he keeps me up. And kicking my bladder must be training to be a great soccer player someday."

They spent the rest of the evening not even watching their binge show. Instead they talked and kissed and kissed and talked. It made for a special evening.

IT TOOK BOTH SPOOKY and Claire working together for the rest of the week to get all of the boxes unpacked and put away. Then the things she'd ordered for the nursery started coming in.

She kept the door closed in the evenings, and she and Claire worked constantly to get the nursery finished. The two of them built furniture and painted the room together. Spooky wanted desperately to do the work herself, and it would be easier to get forgiveness from Chase than permission.

At the end of her third week of marriage, the nursery was done. She had even put diapers onto the changing table.

When she showed Chase for the first time, he smiled. "I knew you were working on this. Please tell me you let Claire paint it."

"More like we did it together." Spooky walked into the room and touched the huge Mickey decal on the wall. "I love how it turned out."

"I do too. It's a cozy room for Goblin."

"We really do need to sit down and go over names," she said. "I don't want to give our son Goblin for his real name."

Chase laughed, loving how she spoke about the baby belonging to both of them. "I don't think Goblin is what we want the world calling him. What about Jacob? He was my first ancestor to move here."

Spooky smiled. "I like that. We'll make a note of that name, and if we don't come up with another we like better, we'll use Jacob. We could also call him Jake."

Chase grinned. "You know we're probably just going to call him Goblin anyway, right?"

"I do. I hope the whole town doesn't though. Having a name like Spooky has taught me that nicknames can be very hard to explain."

"I'm sure. I know I thought it was crazy when you told me your name was Spooky. I understand now, but Goblin might be even harder to explain."

"When we figure out what he'll be called, we need to put his name on the wall in the nursery. Then I'll feel that it's totally ready for him."

"Have you gotten clothes yet?" he asked.

She shook her head. "I mean a few cute things, but I need sleepers and everyday clothes for him. Not just church clothes."

"That's true. Do you want to plan a trip to Pocatello on Monday? There's this great Thai place with the best yellow curry you've ever tasted."

"I'm in!" She grinned at him. "I want to get other sizes of diapers as well, if you don't mind. It would be really nice not to have to run out like it's an emergency whenever he grows a little."

He shrugged. "I don't mind that at all. We'll put extra things in the closet in his room or even in one of the upstairs rooms if we need to."

"Oh, I'm sure we'll need to. If we get snowed in all winter, I want to have everything we need right here."

"You're scaring me a little."

"We're pretty isolated. I'm not going to risk having nothing for the baby."

"All right." Chase was sure she was going a bit overboard, but it seemed to make her happy to do so, and who was he to complain about having a happy wife?

"Everything is coming together beautifully," she said. "I think I'll even be able to get back to my schoolwork this week."

"Do you have limited time to finish?"

She shook her head. "No, when I realized I was pregnant, I let my faculty advisor know, and she's working with me independently."

"Good!"

"I do want to get as much finished as I can before Goblin is born." She put her hand on the glider rocker there in the nursery, imagining sitting in that very chair, nursing her infant. There was nowhere she would rather be.

THANKSGIVING CAME AND went. They went to his aunt's house, and shared in her feast. Spooky made a dessert. His family was kind to her, but they did tend to look at her stomach more than she would have liked.

Soon they were busy with doctor's appointments every other week. Spooky got a great deal of work done and she was approved to do her thesis on Chase's family history. She loved the idea of being able to research something they would both be interested in.

By Christmas, she was huge. It was hard to do anything, and they opted to stay home and have a quiet Christmas together, rather than spending time with family.

She got Chase some cold weather gear, making certain to use what little money she had when she'd married him. She didn't want him to pay for his own gift on their first Christmas together.

He got her a new computer, having seen hers crash multiple times. She was extremely excited because it had been hard to get her schoolwork done with the old one.

By mid-January, she was ready to do anything to get her labor started and get the baby out. It was too cold to walk outside, so she talked Chase into getting her a treadmill. She felt bad for even thinking about it, but Goblin was about to kill her she felt. She couldn't sleep comfortably, and she just needed to have her body back.

She saw Dr. Miller the day after her due date. "I'm done. Let's do a C-section. Induce me. Use giant forceps and pull him out. I can't do this anymore!"

Dr. Miller laughed. "We all feel that way at the end. I know I did with all three of mine. Would you like to induce on Monday morning?"

Chase's eyes were wide by that point. "Is it more dangerous for her if you induce?"

"No, not at all. Most women choose to be induced these days. And there are a lot of scheduled c-sections as well."

"I would like to induce Monday if we can't do it right this second," Spooky said. "I think if I'm pregnant for even another night I might die."

"Is there any danger of that?" Chase asked, looking concerned.

"Not at all. She's being melodramatic, because being that pregnant just hurts, and you want it to all be over." Dr. Miller smiled. "Monday, be at the hospital at seven. I'll give you a sheet of instructions."

"I'll do anything," Spooky promised.

As they walked out to the car, he frowned at her. "I had no idea you were so ready for Goblin to be born."

"I'm just done. Done being pregnant and ready to be me again. It's not easy being a human incubator."

Chase smiled at the picture that conjured up for him. "Monday's the day then."

"Yup. Finally."

"Did we ever decide for sure on a name?"

Spooky shrugged. "Let's go with Jacob. I have the letters to put on his wall at home."

"Sounds good. I can't wait to look into his little face." Chase paused for a moment. "Have you decided if it's all right for me to be in the delivery room with you?"

She nodded. "Yes. I want you there. You should be the first person to hold him."

"I'd love that," he told her, so looking forward to the little person who would be under his protection. It didn't matter that he'd never really been around babies. This child was his, and he loved the idea that their little Jacob would be raised by him. "Do you want to go out for lunch?"

"I don't want to be out in public again until he's born. I'm not kidding when I say I'm done. I'm crabby, and I'm bigger than a house."

"I'll get us burgers from Dan's. Does that work?"

Spooky nodded. "I'll be waiting at home eagerly for it."

He dropped her off, making sure she got inside before leaving to get the food. It would be strange to see her looking differently once the baby was born, but he was turned on by her no matter what. He had no idea how long it would take her to recover from childbirth, but he hoped it wouldn't be more than a week or two.

Spooky went into the house, where Claire was vacuuming. "What did Dr. Miller say?" Claire asked, turning off the vacuum.

"We're inducing Monday morning," Spooky sat down at the table. "Chase is getting us lunch."

"All right." Claire sat down at the table with her. "I'm going to do a really deep clean of the house while you're in the hospital. I'll get some meals made up and stuck in the freezer for weekends, so you don't have to do anything, and Chase doesn't always have to run out and get food."

Spooky nodded. "That sounds good. I just want it all to be done."

Claire smiled. "The first few weeks will be hard as you get used to sleeping when Goblin does. Know that you can call me at any time if you need help with him."

"I'm so looking forward to holding him and nursing him."

"I know you are. It's still hard in the beginning. Trust me."

"All I can think of is not being pregnant anymore. I'm not worried about the delivery. I just want it done."

"You'll do great," Claire said with a smile. "I know Chase is bouncing off the walls with excitement."

Spooky took a deep breath and nodded. "We're going to name him Jacob."

"I love that name. Good choice. Middle name?"

Spooky groaned. "I guess we'll have to figure that out this weekend. How would an official middle name of Goblin sound?"

"Insane."

"That's what I was afraid of."

Chase brought the food in and they dug into the bags, each of them taking their own burger. When he came back in with the shakes, he sat down and joined them. "We only have three days. I really thought it would be longer."

"Three days is more than enough," Spooky said.

"I haven't baby proofed the house yet."

"The baby won't be mobile for months. There's time."

"I can take care of that while they're in the hospital if you'd like," Claire offered. "I plan on doing a deep clean of the whole house."

"It would be much appreciated," Chase said. "I want everything perfect for when Jacob comes home." He felt a bit of pride when he said the name, thrilled they were naming the baby after one of his ancestors.

"Would you mind if we used Douglas as a middle name?" Spooky asked out of the blue. "He'll have your last name, but he needs to have a little bit of his biological father as well."

"Of course, I don't mind," Chase said, but he found he did. He didn't want his son to have anything to do with her first husband. Not even a name.

"That's what we'll do then. I want to be able to tell my former mother-in-law that Jacob will have his father's name as his middle name. They want him to carry his last name as well, but I'm not doing that. He'll have your last name."

"Our last name."

Spooky nodded. As tightly as she'd clung to her maiden name when she married the first time, was as much as she wanted to share Chase's last name. They would be a real family.

Chapter Eight

By late Monday afternoon, Jacob was born and both parents were totally infatuated with their new child. While Spooky slept for a while, Chase just held the baby, looking down into his little face and seeing the most beautiful thing he'd ever dreamed of holding in his arms.

Spooky and Jacob were able to go home on Wednesday afternoon, and Chase couldn't have been prouder of his new family. He was certain he'd texted at least one-hundred photos of his new son to his father by then.

Spooky was recovering beautifully, still sore from the birth, but so happy to have her perfect little boy in her arms and not in her womb. He fussed a little on the ride home from the hospital, and she wished she could hold him in her arms, but she knew better. She wasn't about to be in a moving vehicle with her baby out of a car seat.

As soon as they were in the house, Claire took over Spooky and Jacob's care. She put Jacob into his bassinet and Spooky onto the couch, where she could hear if she needed anything.

But Spooky wasn't thrilled not to have the care of her baby to herself. When he woke up, Claire immediately went to get him, but after a few hours, Spooky said, "Let me do it. I've dreamed of this."

Claire nodded, immediately backing off. "I can get the diapers if that's easier for you."

"No, I even want to do that. You should go home and be with your own children."

"All right. Supper is in the crock pot when you're ready for it. Let me know if you do need anything."

Thankfully, the baby was nursing beautifully, though Spooky pumped every few hours, so she could have a supply in the freezer.

The whole while, Chase hovered. He watched Spooky, and every time she moved a little or flinched, he asked her what she needed. Finally, she looked at him and said, "I need you to go back to work tomorrow. I'm doing just fine, and the doctor isn't worried, so why are you?"

"I don't want to miss any of it," he said.

"All he does is eat, sleep, poop, and sleep some more. There's nothing to miss. I swear, if he stands up and starts dancing, you'll be the first call I make after the news stations."

Chase grinned. "All right. I can see that I'm being paranoid."

"You are, and it's so sweet. But I want to take care of our baby on my own. If it becomes too much, I'll call you, and you can come right home. As is, I'll only have a couple of hours each day without you or Claire here."

"That's true." He walked to the fireplace. "I'm going to add another log to the fire, and then I'll go do some bookwork."

"Sounds like a perfect plan." Spooky was tired, but she felt good. There was no reason for anyone to treat her as if she was recovering from major surgery.

Those first weeks with Jacob were ones Spooky would treasure for her entire life. If she'd had an older child, perhaps she would have needed help, but she didn't. It was just her and her little Goblin, who proved to be just as hungry outside the womb as he had been in it.

Spooky slept in the room she'd been in since her arrival, happy to be able to hear the baby cry during the night. Sometimes, she just let him stay in bed with her after a midnight feeding. Jacob was such a good baby. She couldn't imagine anything better than being his mother.

Her and the baby's six week check up went perfectly. "You can return to all normal activities," Dr. Miller told her before smiling down at the baby. "He's perfect. Is he eating and sleeping well?"

"I think he's going to be a linebacker," Spooky said. "Not only did he practice by kicking my bladder, now all he does is eat."

"He's gaining nicely. How are you and Chase doing?"

"Good. He hovers a little more than I'd like, but he loves the baby just as much as I do."

"A new daddy hovering is actually a good thing," Dr. Miller said. "He cares about both of you deeply." Dr. Miller had been filled in on a little of their story as strangers marrying. "I'm going to need to see the baby in another month. If you have any issues before then, give me a call."

As Spooky carried the baby out to the car, she thought about what it meant to return to all normal activities. Her waist wasn't as small as it once had been. There was still a bit of baby weight in her belly, but it didn't matter. She and Chase would finally be able to make love, and it's something she'd wanted since their first week of marriage.

Jacob was a doll that evening, sleeping through their supper and waking only to eat before going right back to sleep. He had yet to sleep through the night, but it didn't bother Spooky at all. She enjoyed waking and taking care of him.

After he was in his fresh diaper and sleeping soundly, instead of going back out to the living room, Spooky took a long hot bath, afterwards dressing in a simple silk nightgown that stopped at mid-thigh. She'd be cold for a little while, but she had a feeling she and Chase would find a way to warm her up quickly.

"Baby down?" Chase asked when he heard her footsteps.

"Yeah. He's sleeping like a baby."

"That's a good thing, since he is one."

"Very true." Chase had yet to look up from what he was doing on his phone, and Spooky stood and waited. When he did look up, his eyes widened. "You probably need a robe to keep warm."

"Oh, I have a better way to keep warm if you're up for it."

"Oh?" He stood and walked toward her. "I thought we had to wait for six weeks."

She laughed. "It's been six weeks. I had my check up today."

"You should have said something sooner." Chase was more than eager to get her into his bed where she belonged. "We'll leave the doors open in case the baby cries," he said, and that was the last thought he had about Jacob. Now was time to focus on his beautiful wife who he had waited so long to make love with.

Taking her hand, he led her into his bedroom. "You sure you're ready?" he asked. It took every bit of his restraint to ask before pushing her down on the bed and ravishing her.

She nodded. "I've been ready. My body just needed a little time to heal, and it has."

Going against every one of his instincts, he leaned down and kissed her softly, his hands gently pulling her up against him. He'd seen her breasts many times when the baby would look away while nursing, but he had yet to touch her. It was as if he'd spent years saving up for something special, and now it was right in front of him.

"Is there anything I shouldn't do?"

Spooky laughed softly. "You shouldn't keep stopping to ask questions. I've been waiting for this too, you know."

With that, he pulled her little nightdress thing over her head and tossed it on the floor. Picking her up, he deposited her on his bed and quickly stripped out of his jeans and t-shirt.

"What? No strip tease?" she asked.

"Maybe next time." Chase joined her on the bed, kissing her and letting his hands roam over her body. Before, it had felt like her body belonged to Jacob, but now...now it was his.

He didn't take as long as he probably should have before he covered her body with his and made love with her. As he joined them together, he asked, "Tell me if I hurt you." But he knew there was little he could do about it if he did hurt her. He'd waited too long for this moment.

"I don't think you could hurt me if you tried," she responded, her hands stroking his shoulders. She'd always had a thing for shoulders, and though he had a wiry cowboy body, his shoulders were strong and broad.

As they moved together in the oldest act in the world, she knew without a doubt that she loved Chase. There had been little doubt in her mind before, but his tenderness and caring, well, it told her all she needed to know. Her feelings for this man were so much stronger than she'd ever imagined possible.

When they both reached their peak, he rolled to his side, gathering her body to bring with him. They were both out of breath, but he pulled her head to his shoulder, and his hands never stopped moving over her.

After a long while, he said, "That was definitely worth waiting for."

She giggled, her hand moving down his body. "Oh, yeah? I thought so too."

He caught her hand before it could reach its ultimate destination. "I don't want to hurt you."

"You didn't hurt me. Not one little bit."

"Good. Because I wouldn't hurt you for the world." He lay holding her, realizing he wasn't ready for sleep yet. "I'm hungry."

She laughed. "There's more of supper, or I could make us a snack."

"Sounds good to me." He got out of bed, stretching, while she watched him. He was aware of her eyes on his body, and he couldn't deny that he enjoyed the look she was giving him. Putting on a pair of clean underwear and his t-shirt he'd just taken off, he looked at her. "I thought you were going to feed me."

She sighed dramatically. "I have two men in my life, and all they want me to do is feed them. I guess I should be happy that you just want me to cook something and not make your meal inside my body."

Chase grinned, reaching down to take her hand and help her out of bed. "We should do that more often."

"After I feed you though, right?"

Nodding, he said, "Well, of course. Maybe you should just plan on several meals throughout the night so I have the energy to do what I want."

"Maybe you should plan on nuking something for yourself when you get hungry," she said.

Having no clothes in his room other than her flimsy nightgown, she grabbed his robe from the bathroom and pulled it on, rolling it up to her elbows. "All right. Let's see what we can find for a snack."

He followed her to the kitchen, sitting on one of the stools to watch her cook. Now that he'd felt every inch of her body, watching her was more of a turn on than ever. "Anything works for me. I'm just hungry."

She opened the freezer and saw a couple of frozen pizzas. "Pizza?" she asked.

"That's good energy food," Chase said. "Sounds delicious."

She preheated the oven and moved to sit beside him on one of the other stools. "It'll take a little while."

"But I'm starving."

She rolled her eyes. "Did you work up an appetite?" Kissing him was easy and so natural. She'd had to think about everything before she did it with Doug. Everything seemed right with Chase.

As she was putting the pizza in the oven, he heard a whimper and went to get the baby, changing him and carrying him to her to eat. They moved to the couch, and he couldn't believe how sexy he found it when she just moved one side of the robe she was wearing out of the way and put the baby to her breast.

"I like it when you wear my clothes," he said.

"Don't get used to it. I tend to prefer my own." She'd worn little but sweat pants and t-shirts since the baby was born, but he didn't seem to mind at all.

"I guess that's okay." He couldn't take his eyes off their son's mouth as it drank greedily from her breast. "He's going to be huge if he keeps eating the way he is."

She laughed. "He's already at the top of his percentile in both height and weight."

"Soon we'll make another. Maybe a girl this time."

"Let's enjoy this one for a little while before we rush to have another."

"He needs a swing set. And a playhouse."

"He needs to crawl before he enjoys either of those things." She was putting him down on the floor for tummy time often during the day, and though he didn't seem to care for any of his toys yet, she knew he soon would.

When he was finished eating, Jacob immediately went back to sleep, and though they both knew that wouldn't happen often, it was nice that he was giving them that night alone.

While she got the pizza from the oven, Chase carried Jacob back to his crib. "I hope you know how much I love you and your mama. I won't ever let anything bad happen to either one of you," he promised.

Resting the baby on his back, he stared down at him for a moment, returning to the kitchen to find Spooky already eating. "Hey, you started without me!"

"I'm making food in my body to sustain another human. I need nourishment," she said unapologetically.

"Well, you wore me out earlier. I think you vampired all my energy, and now you need to add it back."

She shook her head. "I fixed you a plate. Have at it."

Their easy banter made her so happy she couldn't even express it. She had no idea what she'd done in her life that was so good she deserved a man like Chase, but whatever it was, she needed to be sure she kept doing it.

Having a man who accepted both her and another man's baby so completely...well, it brought tears to her eyes, and she didn't want him to see them. Ever. It wouldn't be a good idea at all to let him know how very important he was to her. That would give him too much power over her, and she didn't need this to turn into another marriage like her first.

As they ate their pizza together in silence, she made a silent vow to never let him know how much she loved him. Ever.

Chapter Nine

It was late May before the snow finally melted and Spooky could start taking Jacob for walks. She'd decided to keep him in for the most part throughout the winter, not wanting to expose him to the flu, let alone whatever new strain of Covid was out there.

She started taking him to the park once a week so she could walk around the track there, and push him in his stroller. At first, he acted like the sun was going to kill him, cringing away from the bright light. For their second walk she made sure she had sunglasses and a little hat for him that would shield his eyes.

When Chase came in at the end of the day, and he saw the tiny sunglasses and hat, he looked at Spooky. "I've never seen a baby in sunglasses."

She shrugged. "I guess he's a vampire and not really a goblin. You should see his reaction to the light."

Chase laughed, taking the baby from her arms and kissing her cheek. "I love how much more alert he is now."

"Me too!" Spooky said. "He's getting a real personality. He'll be crawling in a couple of months, and then our lives as we know them will truly be over." While Chase held Jacob, she spread a blanket on the floor beside the table so he could have tummy time while they ate. She'd already given him his supper consisting of breast milk and rice cereal.

As they ate, Jacob jabbered nonstop. "I'm ready for him to start talking to us," Chase said.

She laughed. "Be careful what you wish for. When he starts, he may not stop."

"I can't wait for my dad to meet him. And Mrs. Turner of course. Who is now my stepmom, but I can't think of her as anything but Mrs.

Turner. I think she's going to be the best grandmother ever." Chase secretly wished they could have an overnight away from the baby. He loved him with everything inside him, but he wanted time alone with his wife. Time they hadn't had since before Jacob was born. He didn't feel free to be a husband and lover when she was always ready to jump up to be Jacob's mother.

"I hope so. It'll be nice to have someone other than the two of us doting on him. I'd always pictured my mom right there for any children I had."

"Do you still have a ton of breastmilk stocked up?" he asked.

"Oh, yeah. The freezer overflows with it. Just this week, Claire put most of it in the garage freezer, so we'd have room for other things in here."

"What would you think of seeing if Dad and Mrs. Turner are willing to play grandparents for a weekend? He'll take a bottle as long as you're not in the room, so I don't think it'll be a big deal."

Spooky frowned. She knew eventually she'd have to be separated from Jacob at least for a little while, but it just didn't feel right yet. "I don't know. I can't imagine him being anywhere else for even a night, let alone a weekend."

Chase nodded, feeling a bit like she didn't care to be with him. "I just thought it might be nice for us to have some real alone time where we're not listening for any little whimper."

Her eyes widened. "Are you starting to resent Jacob?"

"No! I love him with everything inside me. I just...well I just want some time where I don't have to worry about anything. Where we can maybe go to a nice hotel somewhere and enjoy each other."

She understood what he was asking and why, but she hated the idea of not being with her son. "What if he gets scared and we're all the way in Utah?"

"We could try one night just staying here and they'd be in their little house," he suggested. "Then if you were needed, you'd be right there."

"When will they be here?" Spooky asked, trying to think about taking little steps toward his goal of going away.

"Next week. Dad has talked about nothing but seeing his new grandson, and since they're so eager to see him, I thought it would be good if we let them take the time to really be grandparents."

"I'll think about it." It was all Spooky could bring herself to promise him.

"Thank you. I know it frightens you, but as you get to know them, I know you'll feel like I do. You'll be ready to share Jacob with them whenever they feel like taking a turn."

Spooky nodded, but she wasn't so sure. The little boy lying on the floor near the table was her whole world. How could she trust someone enough to love him the way she did? Other than Chase of course, but no one could compare to the love of a mother.

"My dad started building a sunporch last year," he said, changing the subject completely. "It was never finished, but I thought we could put in a hot tub and sauna."

"And an intercom so we can hear the baby?" she asked.

"Of course, an intercom. And we'd only use it after he was in bed."

"I sure like the idea of soaking. Maybe I could read in there."

He nodded. "I'd love that. And I thought we'd put in a porch swing on the back deck. As well as a child's swing."

"You don't worry that Jacob could slip through the rails of the deck?"

"I don't. Because I know we'd watch him better than that, and he would have his own swing to use." Chase wanted her to be a bit freer with Jacob. He felt she was too doting, if such a thing were possible.

"Let's look at some and see what we think."

"And I want to get him a pony. I can't believe he's four months old, and I haven't had him on a horse yet."

Her eyes widened. "You don't think you're going to put him on a horse alone, do you?"

"No. But I can train the pony. And we'll get Jacob used to him. Get him to where he likes the horse. He's going to have to ride like his father does."

"But not til he's older."

"He could sit in the saddle in front of me now. And then by the time he's four or so, he'd be able to be on the pony on his own." He knew it's how his father had raised him, and many children in the area had been raised the same way. "We'll have him ready for the junior rodeo by the time he's ten."

"Rodeo! Rodeos are dangerous."

"They can be," Chase said. "But he's growing up in a world where his father knows a great deal about horses. I rode in junior rodeo, and so did all my friends. You need to stop worrying."

"You're talking about putting my four-month-old baby on a horse. How could I not worry?"

It was her use of the word "my" with regard to Jacob that bothered him. Never before had she indicated that she didn't consider Chase the baby's father.

Chase nodded but said little else. If she was going to be Jacob's only parent, then there was no point in him talking until he was blue in the face, was there?

As soon as they were done eating, Spooky gave Jacob his bath, surprised that Chase didn't join them. Usually he was there for every bath, and he read a story to the baby before she nursed him to sleep.

When Chase didn't come into the nursery to read a story, Spooky chose one and read it to him softly. She couldn't wait until he was old enough, she could teach him to read. Books were an important part of her life, and she wanted him to feel the same.

Slipping the baby into his crib, she went out into the living room and sat with Chase on the couch. He was watching a show that she'd never seen and looking down at his phone. "What are you watching?" she asked.

He shrugged. "Just a show I used to watch. Thought I'd catch up on it while you were busy." But he made no move to change to the show they were watching together.

She sat there for a while, waiting for him to say something to her, but when he didn't, she finally stood. "I'm going to take a long hot bath and go to bed." Usually she just took a shower in the morning or a bath while the baby slept. It was odd for her to bathe at night, because she wanted to spend every minute she could with him.

He nodded, but said nothing, so she went to their bathroom and filled the tub. She never really took the time to fill it with bubbles but she did, and she took a book into the bath with her.

She lingered for more than an hour in the tub before getting out and getting ready for bed. When she looked, Chase was still in the living room watching television. They'd never gone to bed separately, so his behavior was very odd to her. "I'm going to bed now," she told him.

He nodded, again not looking up. Whatever his problem was, she knew he was upset with her, but she couldn't imagine why. Climbing into bed alone felt strange to her, but there was nothing else to do. She read another chapter, and then she fell asleep, wondering when Chase was going to come to bed.

When she woke the following morning, the other side of the bed was untouched. She walked into the living room and found Chase sprawled out on the couch, sound asleep. Putting her hand on his shoulder, she said, "It's time to get up."

He jerked awake, rubbing the sleep from his eyes. "Thanks." He never made eye contact with her as he went to their room to shower and dress for his day.

Breakfast was the one meal she made every day, so she went into the kitchen and made pancakes with bacon, knowing it was his favorite, hoping whatever she'd done, she hadn't made him regret marrying her.

Chase thought for a moment about going straight to work and not bothering with breakfast, but he knew better. He needed nourishment to make it through the day, especially during calving.

When he sat down at the table and started eating, Spooky watched him. "We'll let your dad and Mrs. Turner take Jacob for a night while they're here, and if it goes well, we can go away for a weekend." It still frightened her, but if that's what he was upset about, she wanted the problem gone.

"It doesn't matter. Whatever you feel is right for your child." Chase wasn't going to discuss it all over again. He just wanted to forget everything she'd said.

"My child?" she asked, surprised. "I thought he was our child?" When had he decided Jacob wasn't his? It was like a slap in the face.

"I thought so too." He got to his feet, slammed his hat on his head, and left the house without another word. He wasn't going to feel like an intruder in his own home.

Spooky thought back about their discussion the night before and tried to remember if she'd said anything about Jacob being hers and not Chase's, but she couldn't remember the exact words of the conversation.

Now she knew she needed a sitter, and she didn't want to wait the week for his father and Mrs. Turner to come back.

Claire was there a few minutes later, and Spooky asked something she hadn't ever expected to ask of her housekeeper and friend. "Are you busy tonight?"

Claire looked at her with a frown. "Not really. The kids are out of school in a couple of days, and the excitement is high in my home, but I'm all for getting away from there."

"Could I get you to watch Jacob for me? I think Chase and I need a night out without the baby." As hard as it would be to leave Jacob, Spooky knew she was making the right decision. Her marriage was too important to her to let Chase stay angry with her.

"Of course. This is a big step. Are you sure you're ready?"

"No!"

Claire laughed. "It'll be fine. What are you planning on doing?"

"I thought we'd go to supper in Fish Haven. Maybe go look at the lake."

"With the mosquitos, you certainly don't want to go into the water, but that sounds nice. Make sure to take mosquito spray for you and Chase, though." Claire acted like it was perfectly normal for her and Chase to go out, and that eased Spooky's mind a bit.

Truly, she didn't know of any mother with a four month old child she had never left behind, and she knew she was being overprotective. It was just that Jacob was hers. Never in her life had she had something she loved so much. Except maybe Chase.

Spooky spent the day with Jacob, her mind always on her night out with Chase. She chose one of her favorite outfits that finally fit, and was wearing it by the time Chase came home. She had already nursed Jacob and fed him his cereal, so he was ready for a night of excitement with Claire.

"Claire is going to watch Jacob tonight. I thought it would be nice for us to have a night out."

Chase looked at his wife skeptically. "We don't have to. I know you don't think you should leave him."

"I also don't think I spend enough time alone with you. Balancing motherhood and being a wife can be difficult at times."

He shrugged. "All right. I'll change."

Spooky's heart cried out, "But I love you just the way you are." Her lips stayed silent though. They would talk at supper and sort everything out or their marriage would fail. As far as she was concerned, it was that simple.

As Chase came out of the bedroom, looking like the handsome cowboy he was, she felt her heart skip a beat.

If she couldn't turn things around, she had no idea what she'd do. Her heart had been hurt when she'd lost Doug, but losing Chase would break it into little tiny pieces that would never go back together again. Not for as long as she lived.

Chapter Ten

Chase led her out to the car, opening her door for her by habit. He wasn't about to be rude to his wife, but he didn't know where he stood with her any longer. From the beginning he'd felt like they'd been of one accord, each of them wanting the same thing, and suddenly it was as if she belonged on another planet. She may as well grow a third breast with as different as she was being!

As they drove toward Fish Haven and the restaurant where they'd gone for their first meal out together, she thought about what she wanted to say to him, so she could find out what was going through his mind.

"I don't like things being awkward between us," she said softly.

"You brought that on yourself," he replied.

"How? I don't know what I said that makes you angry?"

At a stop light, he looked at her in surprise. "Really?"

"Really. I know you want your dad and Mrs. Turner to have Jacob spend the night, and I've already agreed to that. I'm sorry I'm so protective of him. I know I go overboard at times."

"It's not that you're overprotective. What has me upset is that you called him your baby. Since the day we married, he's been our baby. Suddenly he's yours when you don't like what I think we should do. Why is that?"

"I..." And then she realized what she'd said that triggered him so badly. "I didn't mean it that way. I think of you as his father, and I know you think of him as your son."

"Yeah? So I'm his father. What am I to you?" He was tired of the way they never spoke of their feelings for one another. If he was going to be her husband and the father of their son, he needed the words.

"You're my husband."

"I see. Your husband."

"Are you not?" Spooky was getting confused.

"I'm your husband because we stood at the front of a church and said our vows. But do you care about me only because I've agreed to be Jacob's father? Or am I the only one with real feelings?"

"Real feelings?" she asked, afraid of where the conversation was heading.

"Yes, real feelings. I've been in love with you since well before Jacob was born. I'm tired of feeling so much, and you enjoying lovemaking, but never asking how I feel or telling me how you feel. I love you, you ridiculous stubborn woman!"

For a moment, Spooky sat stunned. Then a slow smile spread across her face. "I love you too, Chase. I have for a long time."

"You do?" Chase found the first place to pull over and pulled into a gas station parking lot. "Why haven't you told me?"

She took a deep breath, trying to decide the best way to tell him. "I've been afraid. I was always open with my feelings for Doug, and he with me. But by me telling him I loved him, it was like I almost became subservient to him. I wasn't his equal, and he was quick to let me know that. So when my feelings for you were so much stronger than they ever were for him, I was afraid you'd use my feelings against me."

He sighed. "You need to stop measuring me with the same yardstick you used on that idiot." Chase sighed. "I'm sorry I called him that. But it's something I've wanted to say for a very long time. He messed with you in ways that a man should never mess with a woman." He reached out and traced the curve of her cheek with the tip of his index finger. "You are an incredible woman, Spooky, and you need a man who recognizes that. Who treats you as if you're special in every way. It sounds to me like Doug slowly broke down your self-esteem more each day."

Spooky nodded, a tear drifting down her cheek. "And I never want to be what I became with him again."

"And you shouldn't. You're perfect the way you are now. You're a strong, independent woman, and the mother of a child we both love with everything inside us. But we can love each other as well."

"I'm sorry I was afraid to share how I felt. I really am."

He leaned toward her and kissed her passionately. "Now I want to be home, but I'm taking advantage of date night. It's our first time going anywhere without the baby, and I'm going to enjoy every second of it."

She smiled. "And it's a first step in letting Jacob spend the night without me. I hope you know it has nothing to do with your father or anything you've done. I just don't want to be without *our* baby."

"But you'll try?"

"I'll try." She kissed him once again. "Man, I suddenly understand the appeal of backseats for teenagers."

He laughed. "You never did that?"

"No, we waited until we were married. I think that's probably the only reason he did marry me."

"Well, I'm glad he did because we wouldn't have Jacob without him. And he makes me look really good in comparison."

Spooky laughed. "That he does."

Epilogue

Three years later, Spooky walked outside where Chase had Jacob sitting on his pony and was letting him sit on his own, but ready to catch their son if he needed to.

Jacob loved his pony and all horses as far as Spooky could tell. Chase was the perfect father for a little cowboy.

Spooky walked closer to the corral, two pieces of information needed to be imparted to her husband. She stood just outside the enclosed area, watching her son as he rode in circles. "Can we trot, Daddy?"

"Not yet," Chase said. "Your mama wouldn't like that much. You can trot when you're four."

Jacob looked sad but nodded. "We can't scare Mama."

Spooky smiled. She knew Chase felt like he should be able to do more on his pony, but she just wasn't ready for that, and she was glad he followed her wishes.

"I have news!" she called out.

"Let's ride over to Mama," Chase said, watching carefully as Jacob guided the pony with his knees, holding the reins with just the right amount of strength so Brownie knew Jacob was in charge.

When they reached the fence, Chase kissed her. "And what's your news?"

She held out a piece of paper, and he took it, a slow smile spreading across his face. He showed Jacob, who read it, but didn't seem terribly interested. "It finally came!" she said. "Now I can hang my PhD on the wall, and feel proud of it." She still didn't know if she wanted to work or simply stay home, but the decision would be delayed for a little while by her other piece of news.

"I'm really proud of you. I know it wasn't easy with a little one toddling around."

"No, but he's worth more to me than all the degrees in the world." She grinned. "And I have another piece of news. I think you'll like this one even more."

"Your mother is finally coming for the visit she's been talking about since we got married?"

Spooky laughed. "I've given up on that. I'll believe it when I see it."

"Okay, so what's your news."

"We're having another baby."

Chase gaped at her for a moment. "Really? I thought you were going to take the pill until you finished school."

"I did."

He grabbed her and kissed her again, more excited than he could ever express. "Jacob, you're going to be a big brother."

"I teach baby to ride my pony."

"I think we'll get baby his or her own pony."

"I want brother."

Spooky laughed. "Well, my little goblin, we have to leave that up to God and see what he gives us."

Jacob seemed to think about it and nodded. "Okay."

Spooky would always remember the look of shock and excitement on Chase's face when she told him they were expecting again. And she knew he would always love Jacob as much as any child that was biologically his. With two children, they would feel as if their family was complete. Unless they wanted more...